ROSS OF SILVER RIDGE

Ross Trent wanted a nice cosy middle-aged
woman to take charge of the three young
children in his care – but instead he got
Taryn Bartlett, who was twenty but looked
five years younger. Ross was not pleased,
his glamorous girl-friend Coral was even
less pleased. How long would Taryn last ?

Books you will enjoy
by GWEN WESTWOOD

SWEET ROOTS AND HONEY

Perry was somewhat taken aback when
she discovered that Fabian Sinclair,
whose expedition to the Kalahari desert
she proposed to join, did not expect a
female to come along. 'I see you have
plenty of spirit,' he said, 'and you will
need it.' What was she to do to win the
respect of such a man – and to win his
love?

CITADEL OF SWALLOWS

Stacey was in Greece to visit Colin
Hamilton whom she had been expecting
to marry – but soon found herself more
and more disenchanted with Colin and
more and more interested in the disturbing
Greek Stavros Demetrios. But there the
matter looked like resting, for how could
Stacey hope to interest Stavros, when
Colin's glamorous sister Lauren had
already set her sight on him?

ROSS OF SILVER RIDGE

by

GWEN WESTWOOD

MILLS & BOON LIMITED
17-19 FOLEY STREET
LONDON W1A 1DR

First published 1975
This edition 1975

© *Gwen Westwood 1975*

ISBN 0 263 71899 9

Made and Printed in Great Britain by
Cox & Wyman Ltd, London, Reading
and Fakenham

CHAPTER ONE

'You here again? Taryn Bartlett, isn't it?' said the lady with the high-piled red-tinted hair in the employment bureau. 'You don't last long, do you, dear? What was wrong this time?'

'I couldn't get interested. I'm sorry, but it was too boring.'

Taryn swept back her soft brown hair that she wore to her shoulders. It was always falling across her eyes, those brown eyes that seemed too large for her small face. In her plain shabby suit, she did not look older than fifteen, but she had said she was twenty when she had given her particulars to the redheaded owner of the bureau. Mrs. MacTavish ripped a sheet from her typewriter in an enviably efficient way and shook her head in reprimand.

'With your lack of qualifications, you can't expect excitement. You said you liked books, so I thought this job as a proof-reader would suit you.'

Taryn tried to look apologetic, but instead smiled, and this changed her small pale face into one that had an elusive attraction.

'So did I, but I didn't realize that the proof-reading would mean that I had to read the same letter over and over again. It was a direct mail firm and they sent out hand-typed appeals for funds. Anyhow, it didn't seem honest to me. They had a machine for making the signatures look handwritten.'

'Really, dear, you can't afford to be fussy in business. That's three posts you've turned down. What do you expect me to do for you now? You speak well and look refined, but you must admit you haven't got much training.'

'I know, but I'm alone in the world now. I can't afford to train for anything yet. What would I live on? I think I told you that I gave up my nursing training to look after my grandparents and they both died within a few months of each other. They only had their pensions and I was left with nothing.'

'Yes, yes,' said Mrs. MacTavish, brushing the explanations aside impatiently. 'But the question is what can I find for you now? What about a domestic post?'

'I suppose I could do that,' Taryn replied doubtfully, 'but I've had two years of domestic work. Couldn't you find me something more exciting? My grandparents were loves, but I was tied down. I used to dream of travelling. I'd love to see some other part of the world.'

Mrs. MacTavish made a noise that sounded like a snort.

'I suppose you imagine yourself being companion to some rich old lady, just sorting out her jewels and light work like that. Oh, yes, I have plenty of people coming in here wanting jobs of that kind, but I didn't think it of you, Miss Bartlett.'

'No, truly, if I found something interesting I should be willing to work hard. It's the monotony of the office work that gets me down. I wouldn't mind looking after someone if I could see new places.'

'And how often do you think a job where your travelling is paid for comes up?' said Mrs. MacTavish impatiently. 'Now here's a job that might suit you if you say you don't mind work. You have to look after a five-year-old girl, three-year-old twins and a one-year-old baby. The mother's on telly and doesn't come home until late, so you don't have much time off. Excuse me, dear.'

She lifted the phone which had started to ring loud and shrill. A conversation followed which seemed to consist on her side of dismayed exclamations.

'I wish you could have let me know before this. It's very late to say you can't go. I know Mr. Trent was relying on you. He phoned this morning all the way from South Africa to make sure that everything was in order. Oh, well, it can't be helped, I suppose.'

Her eyes fell on Taryn and their expression changed from one of frowning impatience to that of someone who has suddenly had an idea. She rang off abruptly.

'Well, there you are. There's your chance to travel.'

'What do you mean?' asked Taryn.

The manner of the redheaded lady had changed miraculously. She was beaming at Taryn as if all her disapproval had vanished.

'That wretched woman has let me down at the last moment. She was supposed to travel to South Africa with three children tomorrow, and now she says she can't go because her mother has been taken ill. But here you are, and you say you want to travel. Aren't you lucky?'

She threw the beaming intensity of her rather protuberant eyes on Taryn as if trying to hypnotize her.

'But ... but ... what is the job? What am I supposed to do?'

Now that the chance had presented itself, she was not at all sure that she wanted it. It was all very well to talk grandly about travelling, but rather frightening when one's vague dreams became reality with such startling suddenness.

'Let me look at my files. Yes, here we are. Three children. It won't be difficult, dear, because they're not very young – Melinda, fifteen, Damon, thirteen, and Adrian, eight. They have no mother and their father has had to go to the Far East for two years. An old aunt who has been looking after them can't do so any more, so the father's brother is taking them over and they're to go to some place in the mountains until they're ready for school. Ross Trent, that's his name, wants someone who will travel with the children and stay a while looking after them and doing domestic jobs until they're settled. He has a housekeeper and servants, so it shouldn't be hard work. He'll meet you in Durban. It will be quite a holiday for you. I wouldn't mind going myself. I must say I quite envy you the opportunity.'

'But ... tomorrow! How can I get ready in time?'

'Easy. You won't need much.'

I haven't got much, thought Taryn. She had been staying in a small boarding-house and all her worldly possessions were in one small suitcase. She could leave what she did not need with a friend.

7

'Have you got a passport?'

'Yes.'

Taryn had been planning to walk with a friend in France if they ever got the opportunity. She made a point of keeping her passport up to date.

'And you have the necessary health certificates?'

'I think so.'

'You'd better go and fix it all up this afternoon.'

'I haven't even said I would go,' Taryn protested.

'But you will,' wheedled the overwhelming Mrs. Mac-Tavish. 'Just think of it. While we're going into the cold weather, you'll be basking in the sun. Funny place. They have midsummer at Christmas out there, I believe.'

She phoned various offices and arranged about the transfer of the ticket while Taryn waited and wondered whether she was being incredibly foolish.

'Where do I meet these children?' she asked suddenly recollecting that she did not know a thing about the arrangements.

'Their aunt is bringing them to Victoria air terminal. You'll catch a bus to Heathrow from there. You'll be in Johannesburg next day and catch a connection to Durban. Don't worry. It's very simple.'

It was not difficult to recognize her charges at the air terminal. Melinda, the girl, wore a grey flannel school suit and a sulky expression. The two boys were in conventional English suits, the elder one in long trousers and the younger one in shorts that came to his knees. Damon, the elder, was a handsome dark boy, unlike his sister, who had a ponytail of blonde hair and large blue eyes. She was a very pretty girl, but her mouth had a downward droop at this moment. She looked anything but pleased to be setting out on her journey. The younger boy had her fair colouring and was an attractive clean-looking little boy with radiant English colouring. An elderly woman accompanied them, and when Taryn approached them she looked at her as if she could hardly believe her eyes.

'I'm Taryn Bartlett, Miss Trent,' said Taryn, extending her hand. 'Mrs. MacTavish sent me.'

Miss Trent, who had been looking harassed in any case, now looked even more worried. She ignored Taryn's hand and exclaimed: 'But I told Mrs. MacTavish we needed someone responsible! You look about eighteen.'

'I'm twenty and I'm quite responsible,' Taryn said firmly. Living for some years with her grandparents had made her used to dealing with elderly people. 'Please don't worry about the children. I trained for a while as a nurse and I can assure you that I shall take the utmost care of them.'

Melinda shook her ponytail.

'There you are, Aunt Susan, I told you it wasn't any use employing a stranger to take us. I could have managed perfectly well by myself. I hate being treated like a child! You don't seem to realize how humiliating it is to have to go to meet Ross in charge of a nanny as if we were all Adrian's age.'

'Now don't start this again, Melinda. It's far too late to change anything now. I'm sure Miss Bartlett will be very good company for you. It was just that I was expecting someone older. And you know perfectly well that Ross would never have let you travel alone.'

'Well, for goodness' sake don't come with us on the bus. I'd rather get it over here if you're going to get weepy.'

Taryn thought Miss Trent would be foolish if she got upset over leaving such a rude young girl. It seemed a poor prospect if this was how Melinda was behaving at the very beginning of the journey. But it was too late to change her mind. She was glad when they had disposed of their luggage, boarded the bus and were on their way through London. Adrian and Damon sat in front and she sat next to Melinda, who seemed a little more gracious now that she had left Miss Trent.

'Aunt Susan always fusses so,' she said. 'Of course she's really our great-aunt and about a hundred years old. She knew my father and Ross when they were little boys, and to hear her talk they were absolute paragons. I bet they weren't! I can't imagine Ross doing as he was told if he didn't want to do it.'

'Have you met him, then?' asked Taryn.

9

'Yes. He came to see us a few times. He's fabulous. Women adore him – terribly good-looking, gorgeous tan and navy blue eyes.'

'Good heavens!' said Taryn.

'But you needn't think just because you're taking us there that he'll take much notice of you. The women he likes are the glamorous, well-dressed kind, and you're hardly that, are you?'

'No,' Taryn agreed amiably.

She was not going to allow this obstreperous young girl to deflate her. She was beginning to feel excited now. They were sitting on the top deck and she looked around to see what kind of people would be travelling with them. They all looked fairly ordinary. And yet surely they must feel as excited as she did that they were going to get on a plane and be whirled to distant strange places. Mrs. MacTavish had been right in one thing. Travelling was simple enough. They were soon installed in their comfortable seats and Taryn had ended the dispute between Damon and Adrian about the window seat by suggesting that they should take it in turns to sit there. As soon as the plane stopped acting like a high-speed lift heading straight for heaven and levelled out, it was just like being in a train that was running on lines of smoothest silk.

Soon Adrian was reading the comics that he had been clutching and Damon was engrossed in a book. Melinda, her peevish expression gone for the time being and her lovely face turned sideways to Taryn, was far away in some private dream. Miss Trent at the moment of parting had thrust a compendium of games into Taryn's hand, but she would keep it for later.

Up to now she had hardly had time to think of the implications of her sudden decision to accept this commission to accompany the children and she still felt buoyed up by excitement. She was not afraid that she would not be able to cope with the travelling part of it, for up to now everything had gone smoothly. But what lay ahead? One could not go by the opinion Melinda had expressed of Ross Trent, their guardian. If he was their relation, and a young one at that, of course he would appear glamorous to a young girl, especially since he was apparently rich and lived in a strange, exciting land. Taryn decided she would reserve judgment on him even if Melinda had given the impression that he was something of a playboy.

They all slept well and the night was almost over when Taryn went to accompany Adrian to the washroom. She stood near a window waiting for him and noticed that in the east there was a glimmer of light. Down below the clouds were still dark, but suddenly the sun appeared above the horizon.

'Look,' she said to Adrian, who had joined her. 'You can see the earth curving towards the sun. You can actually see that the earth is round.'

Adrian was very thrilled with this and they spent some while watching as the sun rose higher and the light fell in rosy colours upon the nearer clouds. The world below them was still in darkness under a blanket of dark clouds that looked like an ocean.

At last they reached Johannesburg and found there was a little time to wait before they could catch the plane to Durban.

'It might be a good idea if we all went to make ourselves a bit tidier,' Taryn suggested. 'I think your uncle would appreciate your looking your best when you arrive.'

'You don't think we call him Uncle, do you?' said Melinda scornfully. 'He likes us to call him Ross. And if you think I'm going to meet him in this school uniform, you can think again! I've got another outfit in my vanity case and I'm going to change into it whatever anyone thinks.'

Taryn let her have her way. They were all weary and tired from the journey and she did not want to start a quarrel at this stage. In the rest room, Melinda produced a faded pair of jeans and a brief top of cotton jersey. Having dressed in these garments, she proceeded to make up her eyes with shadow and mascara and to paint her lips in a rather violent raspberry colour. Taryn thought she would leave it to Mr. Trent to raise any objections. She herself would be glad when they reached the end of the journey. She looked at her

11

own reflection in the mirror. Pale, and with no make-up, she looked younger than Melinda. Her brown suit with the cream-coloured blouse looked something like a school uniform and her soft brown hair fell in dishevelled waves around the small heart-shaped face. She remembered that she had a few hairpins in her bag, and combing her hair back from her brow twisted it up in a knot. It was so fine and silky that it did not arrange very easily in this way, but at least she had the satisfaction of knowing she looked a little older.

Damon jeered when he saw his sister.

'I suppose you think you look great. Why did you let her put all that lipstick on, Taryn? Ross will think you're mad!'

Melinda's eyes flashed. She was really a most beautiful girl, thought Taryn.

'He won't! Ross likes girls to use make-up. I know he does. He's not like Aunt Susan. We're going to have a wonderful time living with Ross. I'm free now, and no one is going to boss me around.'

'Now calm down, both of you. That's the call for the Durban plane,' said Taryn.

Less than an hour later, they landed at an airport that was smaller than the one in Johannesburg. Taryn's first impression was one of heat. As they walked from the plane, the sky was a vivid blue, glittering with sunshine. She caught a glimpse of dark-skinned Indians, the women dressed in graceful, colourful saris. But Melinda tugged at her arm.

'There's Ross. You can see him easily because he's so tall. Hold this bag, Taryn.'

Thrusting her vanity case into Taryn's unwilling hand, she ran towards the tall figure at the gate. Taryn, already burdened with her own hand luggage, Adrian's jacket and the compendium of games, felt a lock of hair falling down but could not do anything about it. Clutching Adrian by the hand and weighted with hand luggage, her carefully arranged hair coming down on both sides of her face, she advanced to meet Ross Trent, and looked up in to a face that was darkly attractive. She had been astonished by Melinda's description of 'navy blue eyes', but it was true. She had never seen eyes like them, dark cobalt and with an expression of challenge, rimmed by black lashes, heavy as a film star's. And yet there was nothing feminine about Ross Trent, quite the reverse. The dark brown springing curls, the firm clearcut features, the broad shoulders and slim waist gave an impression of intense masculinity that was emphasized by the even golden tan. It was as if he spent every spare moment soaking up this radiant sun that had struck at them like some glowing fire as they made their way across the tarmac. He smiled as Melinda flung herself at him.

'Ross, it's fabulous to see you again! You haven't changed at all.'

'But you have, young lady, and Damon and Adrian. I would hardly have known you.'

'Oh, don't say all those boring things about how you've grown, Ross. I couldn't stand it from you.'

'Not even if I say you've grown very beautiful, Melinda?'

'Yes, that's allowed.'

Taryn, standing alone and waiting to be noticed, reflected that even at this age Melinda had a sparkling charm that could only grow and become more potent as she grew older. No wonder she was inclined to be headstrong and wanted her own way so much.

'And this is . . .?'

At last the dark blue eyes were turned gravely towards her. She noticed that they widened a little as if he were surprised by her appearance. And no wonder, for she felt anything but neat with her brown hair descending over her collar.

'This is Taryn Bartlett, Ross. I don't know why you bothered to get anyone to come with us. I could easily have brought the boys. I suppose you hadn't realized I'd grown up,' Melinda added excusingly.

Damon snorted. 'You always think you know best, don't you, Melly? I could have looked after myself too. I wouldn't have needed you. She put on all that lipstick specially for you, Ross.'

'Little beast!' hissed Melinda.

But Ross took no notice of this exchange. He was regarding Taryn with a puzzled frown.

'I understood Mrs. MacTavish to say that she had employed a middle-aged woman. You look very far from that description, Miss Bartlett.'

'We call her Taryn,' said Adrian. 'She's better than anyone old. She showed me the sun coming up over the earth. Did you know, Ross, you can really see that it's round?'

'The woman Mrs. MacTavish had engaged couldn't come,' Taryn explained. 'I stood in for her at the last moment.'

'I understand. Well, come along, we'd better do something about getting your suitcases. I thought you might be tired, so we're staying for the night at a hotel on the beachfront and then going on to Silver Ridge tomorrow.'

Taryn felt that she had been judged and found wanting by this man who, with his smart, almost military, safari suit looked as if he could never appear untidy. It was hardly her fault that she looked so young. She would show him that she was competent to do the work required of her. But was she? She did not even know what she would have to do. Probably everything would be different in a new strange land. When she got the opportunity she would ask him what her duties would be.

'What an enormous car,' said Melinda as they came to the silver-grey Mercedes that Ross indicated. 'May I sit next to you, Ross? I feel car-sick in the back, specially when I'm excited.'

'That's just an excuse,' said Damon. 'What a super car, Ross.'

'I'll show it to you properly, young man, when we have more time.'

Taryn thought this was tactful of Ross because Damon was probably envious that Melinda had taken the front seat when he would have liked to examine the dashboard. She took her own place between the two boys, leaving the

14

window seats for them so that they could see the passing scenery well. As usually seems to happen, the airport was situated in a place that necessitated driving through an industrial area, but after a few miles the freeway led them on to an esplanade and at last it was as Taryn had imagined a far-away foreign place should look. On one side there were palm trees, tall and slender, their ragged leaves waving like locks of hair in the wind from the sea. To their left were tall blocks of flats, but on the right Taryn could catch glimpses of a large bay beyond the green stretches of lawn that were ablaze with canna lilies, scarlet, pink and gold.

There were ships anchored in the harbour and yachts scudding along in the breeze, their white sails billowing. Then on past more buildings until at last they were on the beach-front, with more flats and hotels and an impression of light, colour and sound from various cafés and amusement places. Their hotel was right in the middle of all this, an old-fashioned, elegant-looking edifice seeming out of place amongst the huge nursery-rhyme figures and towers of coloured lights just across the road. A uniformed porter ushered them out of the car, and Taryn felt even more untidy as she stood in the round foyer waiting to be shown up to the rooms.

Ross had thoughtfully provided single rooms for herself and Melinda. Taryn was shown to a small room with luxurious wall-to-wall carpeting in deep turquoise, peach-coloured velvet curtains, and a small bathroom in turquoise and pink. Ross had told them not to bother to unpack except for the few things they would need, and that they would be having dinner in his private suite so need not dress very formally. For the first time since she had begun this journey, Taryn found herself alone. Outside the hotel, the bustling life of the beach entertainments went on, but the windows of her suite were closed because of the air-conditioning and she felt solitary and remote from the gay crowds who thronged the sunlit shore.

What was she doing here? Had she been foolish to grasp so eagerly at the chance to get away from the humdrum jobs in London? Whatever she was expected to do in her new post, Taryn felt sure that she would be expected to do it well. Ross Trent struck her as the kind of man who would be a perfectionist. She seemed to be able to get on with the children so far, though Melinda might present some problems. Thinking about this, she nevertheless thoroughly appreciated the deep warm bath that made the water look as turquoise as the sea outside the window.

She changed into a summer dress of a pale floral material in a pretty apricot colour that contrasted well with her dark brown eyes. It was a cheap dress, but becoming, and she made no attempt to put up her hair but let it hang in the natural soft waves that reached to her shoulders. When she was ready she knocked rather timidly at the door that Ross had indicated along the passage and his deep voice bade her to come in. He was alone, standing at the window, his strong profile black against the glittering light of the late afternoon. He turned to look at her.

'Would you like me to go to see how the children are getting on?' asked Taryn, a little unnerved by the intense stare of his dark blue eyes.

'No, no. They've gone to have a bathe in the swimming pool on the roof.'

'But Adrian . . . can he swim?'

'Of course he can. He's been able to swim since he was three. There are plenty of people up there and I asked one of the African waiters to keep an eye on them. Now stop fussing, Taryn, if I may call you that. I'd like to talk to you. Sit down, please.'

Taryn felt at a disadvantage with this tall man as she sat down. He had indicated the window seat and she felt dismayed as he sat beside her, turning to look at her as if, she thought, he were placing her under a microscope.

'I must confess,' he said, 'that I'm rather taken aback by your extreme youth. I especially asked for a middle-aged woman, but I understand the situation and I'm obliged to you for filling in at such short notice. How did it happen that you were free to come?'

Taryn decided that she had better be truthful.

'I'd resigned my office job because I found it too dreary.

16

I'm not well qualified for any kind of work, I'm afraid. I started a nursing career but had to give it up to look after my grandparents. I haven't had a chance since then to do any training because I've needed the money from the work I could get just to keep living.'

'And yet you gave up your job. That doesn't sound very responsible.'

'It may not have been, I suppose,' Taryn admitted. 'But I was fortunate to be offered this opportunity, and it's all very much more exciting than being in an office.'

He frowned a little and she thought she had offended him.

'I know I look young, but I hope you'll find me suitable for whatever you want me to do. I'm quite experienced at domestic work and I like the children.'

He was following his own line of thought.

'I don't know that you'll find this post any more exciting than your last one. I must admit I'm rather disappointed. I'd visualized a motherly type of person with whom I could leave the children when I had to go away, as I often do. If it's glamour you're looking for you may not find it at Silver Ridge. It's really my holiday home, but I felt it would be better for the children to stay there before they go to school. I have a penthouse here in Durban, but naturally, although it's large, it hasn't got sleeping accommodation for a family and Silver Ridge has plenty of bedrooms. I have a house-keeper there and African servants, but I felt she would need some assistance in caring for the children, and I had thought that if you were suitable you could stay on and occasionally help with the domestic arrangements here in Durban. I en-tertain directors who come from overseas on short visits, and the middle-aged person I was expecting could have helped with the catering on these occasions although staying for the most part at Silver Ridge. But of course that's quite out of the question for you.'

'But why?' Taryn protested. 'I'm sure I could cope with these duties if you'd give me the chance.'

'Possibly, but I could hardly expect you to stay alone with me in Durban as I would have expected an older person to do. However, we shall see how things work out. I intend to stay for a while at Silver Ridge until the children are settled. I'm trying to engage a teacher to come and coach them, preferably a man. They're going to go to boarding school eventually for the two years they'll be here, and in any case the syllabus will be different from the one they were used to. Until then, however, and possibly after that, I shall need someone to care for the children. If you feel it's beyond you or if you decide you're not suited to the post, that's easily remedied.'

His disapproval which seemed to amount to opposition made Taryn more determined to try to stay. She had been mistaken in giving him the impression that she wanted excitement. She must try to prove she was sensible and could be responsible in caring for the children.

Melinda came in followed by Damon and Adrian. The boys looked spruce with their wet hair flattened down, and Melinda looked a little girl again, for she had plaited her hair and only applied a little lipstick.

'Can we go and see the beach before dinner,' she demanded. 'It looks fabulous.'

They descended in the lift and Ross spoke to the porter, who went outside and gave a piercing whistle, waving his arms wildly as he called to someone on the other side of the road.

'Who is he calling?' asked the boys curiously, then 'Oh!' For in front of the hotel two huge Zulu men had brought their rickshas to a halt. They wore enormous headdresses of waving coloured ostrich plumes with beaded decorations and huge cattle horns. Their tunics were intricately beaded in gay colours and they had sheepskin gaiters and ankle rattles made from coconuts.

'You three go in the front one,' Ross commanded the children, and although Melinda looked a little sulky, she was forced to obey.

'I think Taryn has had enough of you for a while. She can come with me,' said Ross.

So Taryn found herself sharing the small seat with Ross as the Zulu started off on a wild ride along the promenade.

Every now and again he leapt up into the air with a loud yell, the rattles on his ankles clashing, and the whole vehicle plunging down at the back and skywards at the front. The children were clinging together, squealing with delight, and as Taryn swayed perilously, she felt Ross's arm go round her, holding her tightly to prevent her being flung out.

'It's safer like this,' he shouted, laughing at her startled expression. 'I should have warned you that it's rather an alarming method of locomotion.'

'It's certainly not as smooth as a jet plane,' Taryn agreed.

It was almost dark and suddenly all the coloured lights sprang to life. A huge golden moon was rising over the sea, sending a wide path across the darkening waves. Who would have thought a few days ago that she would find herself riding in this odd fashion in this exciting place? She felt relaxed and happy. This smiling man at her side did not seem intimidating any more. She hoped fervently that she could succeed in pleasing him and could stay in this country that glowed with sunshine during the day and was golden with magic moonshine at night.

'We shall have dinner in my suite,' Ross said as they returned to the hotel. 'It will be less trouble than coping with ordering in the dining-room tonight. And then I think you should all have an early night. I want to start off for Silver Ridge as soon as possible tomorrow.'

'Will you dine with us?' asked Melinda, smiling up at him.

'Of course. Where else?'

'Oh, super!' said Melinda.

She made no attempt to disguise her admiration for Ross. But Taryn was pleased too in a quieter way. Ross had been so much friendlier to her as they rode along the beach front. Laughing and joking, he had lost the serious critical manner that had alarmed her at first. Perhaps she was going to be able to win his approval after all. She sincerely hoped so, for she had enjoyed every second of her adventure since they had started out on their flight to South Africa.

'Don't take long,' Ross shouted to the rest as they went

19

along the corridor to wash their hands and he turned to go in to the door of his suite. As Taryn followed the children who were almost running along to their rooms, she thought she heard a sharp exclamation behind her and then Ross's voice rang out. 'Why, hello, they didn't tell me you were here. This is a pleasant surprise.'

Melinda looked inquiringly at Taryn.

'Someone has come to see Ross. Oh, I do hope whoever it is isn't staying for long.'

'I don't suppose so. It's almost time for dinner.'

'Suppose she stays?' said Melinda gloomily.

'How do you know it's a she?' asked Taryn, rather amused by Melinda's glum expression.

'Sure to be. Ross is so devastating. All the girls were mad about him when he came to see me at school.'

'Well, hurry and tidy yourself and then you can find out,' said Taryn sensibly.

She hoped Melinda was wrong in her surmise, for she had to admit she had been looking forward to dinner spent in Ross's company. But Melinda was right. When they opened the door, there was a low murmur of voices coming from the window seat. In the place where Taryn had had her interview but sitting close together were Ross and a strikingly beautiful girl. Her hair hung to her waist in a fall of ebony silk and her light green eyes contrasted brilliantly with her golden skin. She was wearing a long skirt of some strangely exotic figured silk sweeping to her ankles yet slit so that her perfect bare brown legs were displayed to full advantage with the red-tipped toes encased in sandals of gold with slender straps. Her lovely figure was briefly covered by a halter top that left bare her brown shoulders and small waist.

She glanced up when she heard the door opening and a quick frown spoiled the perfect face that a moment ago had been smiling at Ross with such allure. But she seemed to recover from her displeasure when she was introduced to them.

'This is Coral Swann, a friend of mine.'

Coral smiled an enchanting smile that took in the children

but seemed to ignore Taryn.

'It's good to meet you. It seems we shall be seeing a lot of each other in the future.'

'Coral will be visiting us at Silver Ridge, I expect,' said Ross.

'Why, certainly. And what does Mrs. Fuller think of the additions to your household?'

She smiled up at Ross in such a way that Taryn thought there seemed to be a very intimate association between the two.

'Mrs. Fuller has too easy a time there. It will do her good to have a bit more housekeeping to do. Anyhow, she'll have Taryn here to give her a hand.'

'Oh, yes, of course, Taryn,' Coral turned the blaze of her emerald eyes upon Taryn, who at once felt that her appearance was being analysed and found wanting. 'I thought you said you were getting a middle-aged person to look after the children, Ross.'

Ross explained the circumstances. Taryn was beginning to feel a bit weary of having to apologize for her youthful appearance. She could not remember that it had ever been a disadvantage before.

'So you come from London? I wonder how you're going to like living amongst our wild mountains?'

'I'm looking forward to seeing some more of the country,' Taryn replied.

'It can be rather lonely and boring for a city dweller, can't it, Ross?'

'I've never found it so,' said Ross.

He looked displeased that Coral should be suggesting such a thing.

'It's much better for the children to live there where there'll be walking and riding and they'll be able to have pets.'

'Gosh, it sounds fabulous,' said Damon, but Melinda was gazing in admiration at Coral, seeming to take in every detail of her appearance.

'Do you like it there?' she asked.

Coral laughed with a silvery tinkle that yet had in it a

note of mockery.

'I'm a town girl myself. Personally I think it would be much better if Ross had rented a house in Durban as I suggested. But he's so crazy about wild life and climbing and fishing, aren't you, darling?'

The conversation was interrupted by a knock at the door and a waiter entered with a number of large menus. He handed them around, offering one to Coral. She waved it away.

'I'm glad you've arranged for the children to eat up here,' she said. 'Poor dears, you must be dreadfully tired. But I'm sure Miss . . . Taryn will see that you're not long out of bed. There's a fabulous new place downstairs, Ross. It's just been redecorated and they have a terrific band. I've been longing to try it.'

'But, Ross, you said . . .'

Taryn quickly interrupted Melinda.

'We shall order dinner and then have a game of Scrabble.'

'Yes, do that,' said Ross. Then he smoothed Melinda's fair hair and smiled rather apologetically into the large blue reproachful eyes. 'Sorry, Melinda, our date's off for tonight, but Taryn will look after you.'

'I don't need any looking after,' said Melinda, her mouth mutinous.

'Well, Adrian does, don't you, old man?'

The little boy was sprawled on a chair, his eyes scarcely open.

'We've only just met you, Ross,' Melinda protested. 'I thought you'd be with us for dinner.'

'I shall be with you for lots of dinners in the future. You may think you have too much of my company at Silver Ridge.'

Taryn dined with the children, and in spite of their protests at being sent to bed they were soon asleep. She herself stood on the balcony of her room for a long while gazing at the wide view of the bay, encircled by sparkling lights, so that it looked like a necklace of brilliant jewels. Beyond the lights she could see the dark ocean laced with luminous restless foam, and lighted ships swung restlessly as they waited to enter the crowded harbour.

Her first introduction to South Africa had been to this glamorous place, but she knew that in the morning they would be travelling to somewhere that would be more in keeping with her idea of this wild country. She wondered about Ross. He had spoken in a way that made it plain that he preferred life in the country, and yet Coral had said she was a town girl. But she seemed to have much attraction for Ross, and no wonder, for she was so lovely. He had spoken as if he expected her to come to visit them often. She had been charming with the children even though she had relegated Taryn to the position of domestic help.

And after all, that's just what I am, thought Taryn. So I mustn't be sensitive or disappointed that Ross didn't have dinner with us. I'm as bad as Melinda and have not got as much excuse.

CHAPTER TWO

THE house with its mellow stone walls, golden in the sun, and its steep-pitched thatched roof, looked as if it had grown there against the background of russet grass and huge boulders. They had passed through small towns and travelled upon tarred roads, but for the last few miles the road had become rougher, surfaced in gravel and more winding. At last they had begun to climb steeply, the powerful car taking up all the breadth of the small road so that Taryn wondered what would happen if they met another vehicle.

But all remained peaceful. Above the purr of the engine, she could hear the bubbling murmur of a river on the rocks below. Small partridges and spotted guinea-fowl ran into the grass at the side of the path, and large dark birds rose up with harsh discordant unbirdlike noises. Now at last they had arrived. The house was at the top of a grassy slope and beyond was a background of blue mountain, most oddly shaped and yet beautiful, a range of towering peaks, topped by a few small white clouds.

'The Zulus call the range "Quathlamba", which means Mountain of Spears, but the white man called them "The Dragon" or "Drakensberg",' Ross told the children.

As they drove up to the house, Taryn caught a glimpse of a small lake fed by a mountain stream. Ross waved his hand in that direction.

'One of my interests. That's my private fishing ground,' he said. 'I have a trout hatchery too further down the mountain. We breed them and they come in useful when the cormorants leave us any.'

Upon a few stumps and looking like a Japanese painting were some dark birds with curving beaks and brilliant eyes that scanned the slow ripples of the water, in which their own images were reflected together with the blue sky and fleecy clouds.

There was no formal garden. Grassy slopes led to the

heavy wooden door that was decorated with metal and divided in two like a stable door. A heavy bell hung from a hook and Adrian could not resist touching it. It swung sharply and let out a low musical clang. At that a door within the house banged and a stout figure emerged. This, Taryn thought, must be the Mrs. Fuller mentioned last night. She was plump and rather red in the face. Her mousy hair was pulled back in a tight bun and her expression was marred by a frown. But when she saw Ross it quickly changed and she advanced to meet the little group with a smile that did not seem to reach her eyes.

'Mr. Trent, I wasn't expecting you until later,' she said in a rather flustered manner.

'What difference does it make, Mrs. Fuller? I know you can always conjure up something delicious at a moment's notice.'

This was evidently the way to treat her, for the blatant flattery made her smile a bit more wholeheartedly, but all she said was, 'I know how to do meals for your business colleagues, but I'm not sure I can cater for children.'

'Well, now you'll have someone to help you. I'm sure Taryn here will lend you a hand.'

'Thank you, but I don't need anyone in my kitchen, Mr. Trent. I've always managed very well for you before, as you should know, but I'm not used to children.'

She speaks as if they're some strange kind of animal, thought Taryn. I think she could be a difficult woman. However, we shall see. She glanced around the living-room with its high rafters underneath the thatch, for this room took up the space of the two stories. The floor of glossy light wood was covered with Khelim rugs in shades of autumn leaves, golden, orange, cream, and the deep chairs were of leather in a subtle shade of cinnamon brown. It was a comfortable unpretentious room and yet, if you observed it closely, everything indicated comfort purchased by wealth. There were beautiful pictures, one or two fine pieces of sculpture, and many books lined the shelves beside the big open stone fireplace. It was a masculine room. There was not even a bowl of flowers on the solid wood table in front of the settee.

25

She could not help saying, 'What a lovely room!'

Ross smiled with an easy charm.

'I have quite a few places where I can stay, but I always consider this my favourite home. I guess you could say I'm a countryman at heart, although my interests often force me to stay in the city. Mrs. Fuller seems to have disappeared. I suppose she's preparing lunch, so I'll show you up to your rooms myself.'

A staircase led directly from the huge living-room to the wing of the house that contained the guest rooms.

'The other wing is for my own use,' Ross explained.

There was one room for the two boys, one for Melinda and a separate one for Taryn. Even though they were living in the country, there was every luxury. The bedrooms being right under the thatched roof were of fascinating shapes and each one had its own bathroom. In Taryn's roof dark timber beams supported the white-painted walls and the deep blue carpet matched the Modigliani portrait above the fireplace of a young girl in a blue dress. The bright colours of a handmade patchwork quilt glowed from the bed that had carved wooden corners.

A young African seemed to appear from nowhere and carried the suitcases up the open staircase. He grinned as Ross addressed him in a strange tongue.

'Moses speaks English very well,' Ross informed Taryn. 'You can give him any instructions about things you require to be done for the children.'

Moses clasped both hands together and bowed.

'I am glad to see these young children and Nkosazane.'

Ross laughed. 'That means a young girl. Evidently Moses shares the general impression of your youth, Taryn.'

But Ross was smiling now and did not seem so disapproving. Taryn vowed that she would show him by her responsible actions that it was not a sin to look young. They heard Mrs. Fuller calling to Moses in a harsh voice from somewhere down below and Ross frowned but said nothing. The African bowed again and departed, not hurrying but moving in a dignified fashion. Ross himself left them shortly afterwards, murmuring an instruction to Taryn to make haste and the children could have a tomato juice while she joined him for a sherry before lunch. There was little to unpack, for Taryn had few clothes with her, then she helped the boys and went to see if she could help Melinda.

The room was already chaotic, for the young girl had spread her possessions around so that it did not seem possible that they had had all come from one small suitcase and a hand luggage bag. Melinda seemed to resent her attempt at tidying for her, so she decided it was best to leave it. It was no good arousing the girl's resentment so soon. Taryn sighed inwardly. She was not used to tolerating untidiness. Her months of caring for her grandparents had taught her that it was more efficient to be tidy. Yet she seemed to take the easy way out with Melinda's behaviour all the time. Was she being weak? No, she did not think so. It was much more important to try to gain the girl's friendship.

In spite of Ross's kind words on Mrs. Fuller's cooking, Taryn noticed that the lunch had all come out of tins, but then, as she had said, she had not expected them. Tinned heated soup was followed by tinned meat and a simple salad. Ross hardly seemed to notice what he was eating but responded to the children's chatter and questions with good grace.

'I have to see the chap who's in charge of the trout hatcheries,' he informed them after lunch. 'Who would like to come?'

Of course they all agreed to the plan and Taryn wondered whether she was included or what she was supposed to do. It was all rather vague and the housekeeper seemed unfriendly. She wished Ross had explained what he expected of her. But then he turned to her with that sudden charming smile and said, 'And you, Taryn, do you want to come too?'

She stammered her consent, but he had already turned away and was telling Melinda she must be ready to go in half an hour and to put on stout shoes instead of the frail sandals she was wearing.

'I only have my school shoes,' she pouted.

'Those will do. There's no one to see what you wear here.'

Ross seemed to have got Melinda's measure. With a young girl's vanity, she disliked wearing anything that she thought unbecoming. Taryn went to the boys' room to see what order she could bring there, before they were due to go for their walk. Adrian had unpacked a box of toy cars and was crawling along the passage making the 'vroom-vroom' noises that all small boys seem to make when handling a model car. As Taryn folded shirts to put into the drawers, she became aware of a sudden silence followed by a sharp reprimand, and then Mrs. Fuller appeared in the doorway followed by a crestfallen Adrian.

'I'm sorry, Miss Bartlett, but I simply can't stand this racket any longer. I feel one of my migraines coming on. As I told Mr. Trent, when he said they were coming, I'm really not used to children. And he promised he would engage a competent person to supervise them.'

She was holding her head and she looked at Taryn as if to say she found her anything but competent.

'I'm so sorry, Mrs. Fuller. We're going out for the afternoon, so you'll be able to have a rest.'

The housekeeper smiled sarcastically.

'I suppose you think dinner for six people will prepare itself. Not everyone lands a job in easy street, Miss Bartlett, supposed to be looking after children, but just coming along for the ride, it looks like to me.'

She turned on her heel and slammed the door before Taryn could think of a suitable reply.

'Don't take any notice of her, Taryn, she's an old cow,' said Adrian.

'Adrian, you must never call anyone that!'

'Well, what must I call her, then? I know worse words than that.'

'He does too,' said Damon, who had so far not taken any part in the conversation but had been taking it all in, his dark blue eyes, that were so like Ross's, wide and interested. They both grinned at her and she could not help smiling at them.

'I'm sure Mr. Trent expects you to behave yourself while you're here, and one of the things you can't do is to call

28

people names.'

'Oh, all right, I won't. But if she makes me cross again, I'll say it to myself. There's no law against that, is there?'

With his fair hair and pink cheeks, Adrian looked like a small angel, but the twinkle in his eyes was the essence of a mischievous little boy.

'Are we walking?' asked Melinda, sounding surprised, although Ross had said so before.

'Naturally,' said Ross. 'I have enough driving around in cars in the city. While I'm in the mountains, I walk.'

They set out upon the road, but soon diverged on to a foot path. The distant ranges of mountains were the colour of ripe grapes, but the smaller hills nearby were green and covered with small bushes. The sun was hot in the hollows, but a breeze tempered its sting. High in the sky a bird hovered, seeming motionless in the deep blue air.

'It's a black eagle,' said Ross, following Taryn's glance. 'Glorious birds, proud and free.'

As he lifted his clear-cut profile to the sky, Taryn thought there was something of the eagle in his own fierce direct gaze. She felt an exhilaration she had never before experienced in any other place. Below was the plain with a winding river making its way to the distant sea, but up here the curving hills were backed by jagged peaks dark against the lighter blue of the sky.

The path led downwards and the two boys ran on ahead, but Melinda stayed beside Ross, chattering away to him with a winsome charm that somehow had the effect of excluding Taryn. But she did not care, for she was caught up in the beauty of this rugged countryside, and when a small group of antelope ran with leaping grace across the path and up the slopes, it seemed to complete her joyous feeling that she had come to a place that she could learn to love. After a while they descended to a road again, though it was little more than a track, and arrived at a place where the screen of green weeping willows hid the entrance to the trout hatcheries. Mr. Schroeder, the man in charge, met them at the gate.

'I've brought some visitors for you,' Ross said to him. 'I'm sure they would like to be shown around the hatcheries.'

'That's good. And perhaps you'll join us for tea afterwards? I'll just phone my wife.'

A thatched cottage stood some way up the path a little away from the hatcheries and this was evidently where Mr. Schroeder lived. He proceeded to show them around and Ross came too, asking questions that, Taryn thought, showed he had a more than ordinary grasp of the subject of breeding trout. The children were fascinated, running from one tank to the next, exclaiming at the different sizes. Mr. Schroeder fed them and they leapt out of the water as if they were chickens taking their food.

The cottage was surrounded by great clumps of blue hydrangeas, and Mrs. Schroeder came out of her kitchen drying her hands.

'That's good. You gave me time to whip up a sponge cake,' she said. 'How nice to see you again, Mr. Trent. You've got a fine readymade family, haven't you? But I thought you said there were three, not four.'

She glanced at Taryn in a puzzled fashion. Here we go again, thought Taryn, as Ross introduced her, but Mrs. Schroeder said tactfully, 'How good for these young ones to have someone like you to look after them. Especially here, don't you think so, Mr. Trent? She'll be able to take them around the hills better than some old body you might have engaged.'

Ross did not reply. Perhaps this was a new point of view to him. Taryn thought she was going to like Mrs. Schroeder. She offered to help and they went into the bright kitchen. Copper mugs upon the dresser glowed in the afternoon sun and blue and white cups were set upon a tray. A large sponge cake with a cream and jam filling took pride of place beside them. There was little left to do as Mrs. Schroeder boiled the kettle, yet Taryn felt she was welcome, much more welcome than when she ventured into Mrs. Fuller's domain.

'It must be a great change for a young girl like you who's come straight from London,' her hostess commented.

'Oh, yes, I still feel very bewildered,' Taryn admitted.

'Ah, shame, it's a lovely part of the country for those that it suits. I think Mr. Trent would spend his whole time here if he could, but he has such a lot of different interests. He's a busy man, is Mr. Trent.'

'Does he usually come here with business associates?' asked Taryn, remembering what Mrs. Fuller had said about lunch, but really wanting to ask if he came here a lot with Coral.

'Occasionally, but usually he comes on his own. I think he likes to get away a bit from city life. He had a house party a while ago. A lot of very bright people came. I went to help Mrs. Fuller, as it was too much for her, she said. She's not got overmuch taste for a bit of work. Oh, yes, they were a merry crowd. They turned the house upside down and there was dance music until all hours. But I don't think it was much to Mr. Trent's taste. I think Miss Swann persuaded him to have the party – Miss Coral Swann. She's a well-known fashion model. Have you met her yet?'

'Yes. She was in Durban at the hotel the night we came, last night, in fact.'

'She would be,' said Mrs. Schroeder. 'She takes a great interest in Mr. Trent's life. But I doubt that it would suit her that he's undertaken the care of three children.'

'You don't sound as if you like her very much. I thought she was very beautiful.'

'I'll grant you that. And men don't often see beyond that, do they? But Mr. Trent is a good man. He deserves better than that and I hope he gets it.'

'Good?'

Taryn thought this was a strange thing to say about Ross, who looked strong, self-willed and as if he would not let anything stand in his way. It did not seem likely he would be taken in by any woman unless he wanted to be. But Mrs. Schroeder had poured the boiling water on to the tea and in the flurry of taking the tray into the other room, the conversation could not be continued.

The delicious sponge cake, light as a cloud, disappeared in a few minutes, and afterwards Ross turned to Taryn, saying, 'Do you think you could find your way back with the children? I have a few more things to discuss with Tom here, but it looks as if it might come up to rain a bit later and as yet you're not used to these sudden mountain storms.'

'Of course,' Taryn replied.

The route here had been very simple. It would take longer going back, of course, because it was all uphill.

'Can't I wait for you, Ross?' Melinda demanded, lingering as the others prepared to set out.

'No, my dear. Those shoes are not suitable for wet weather. We must go to the town to find some better walking shoes for you all, I can see. Taryn is the only one properly shod. I'm amazed that a London girl should have such sensible shoes.'

'I'd arranged a walking tour in France. But I came here instead.'

Taryn was surprised that the sun which had gleamed so brightly on the outward journey had now hidden behind the mist that had descended on to the mountain tops. Cloud shadows scudded over the countryside with now and again a fitful gleam from the hidden sun. They walked quickly along the bridle path with the two boys in front and Melinda lagging some way behind.

'Come on, Melinda, the clouds are descending lower. We'd better get going.'

'My shoes are hurting me. They're too small.'

Taryn had not noticed any complaints on the outward walk to the hatcheries. She was sure that Melinda would not have had such a downcast expression if Ross had been present.

'Do try to walk a bit more quickly. I don't want Adrian, or any of us for that matter, to get wet.'

'I'll walk over the hill. It will be quicker.'

'No, don't do that.'

But Melinda had already turned on her heeel and was making her way at a pace that belied her previous complaint up the slope. Taryn was in a quandary. She could not let Adrian walk the way Melinda was going even if it was a short cut, but she was afraid that Melinda might lose her way.

32

'Leave her,' Damon advised. 'You can't argue with her when she's in this kind of mood.'

But when they reached the house just as the first big drops of rain began to fall, there was no sign of Melinda. Mrs. Fuller, in a kitchen that was redolent with the smell of roasting beef, said she had not seen her.

'Surely she should have stayed with you,' she said rather accusingly, and Taryn could not help agreeing, but how did you get a rebellious young girl like Melinda to obey you when she took no notice of anyone else's wishes but her own? Leaving Damon to entertain Adrian with a game, she put on a raincoat and went out on to the slopes of the hillside. A gale force wind had suddenly swept down from the mountain, swaying the tops of the bushes and making progress difficult as the path almost instantly became muddy and the rain drove under her hood, soaking her hair and making it difficult to see more than a few yards ahead.

She had gone on like this for about a mile, slipping and sliding upon the path and looking vainly up the slopes for any sign of Melinda, when down below she saw a truck making slow progress along the road that led to the house.

'That must be Ross,' she thought. 'Mr. Schroeder has brought him home. Now I must tell him that Melinda is missing.' She felt cold with fright and shock as well as with the biting wind. Fortunately they must have sighted her yellow raincoat and the truck drew to a halt. Almost as soon as it stopped, a tall figure jumped down from the cab and came striding towards her. Ross had no coat and by the time they met on the path his thin shirt clung to his body and his dark hair was plastered in wet curls on his forehead.

'Taryn, what the hell are you doing here? I thought you'd all have got back before the storm broke.'

She was so anxious that she found she could ignore his angry expression.

'It's Melinda. She went off on her own. She said she was going to take a short cut, but she must have missed the way, because she isn't at the house.'

To Taryn's surprise, Ross started to laugh.

'So that was her story! She's a brat and no mistake. She

33

must have changed her mind and doubled back to the hatcheries. She's in the truck right now. She said you hurried her too much and her feet were sore.

'We'll both sit in the back of the truck,' he said, when they reached it. 'We're too wet to come inside.'

'Why were you worried about me?' asked Melinda blandly. 'I'm quite old enough to look after myself. Surely you should know that by now, Taryn.'

Her pleased smile made Taryn have a primitive urge to smack her, but she felt it best to keep quiet. At least Melinda did not get all her own way, for if it had been her aim to come home with Ross she must have been disappointed, since she was left alone in the cab with Mr. Schroeder while Ross and Taryn huddled in the back. As they leaned against the rough boards, Ross put his arm around Taryn.

'You don't mind, do you?' he asked. 'It will make you a bit more comfortable.'

She was past caring whatever happened. Wet, bedraggled, and cold, she thought wretchedly that everything she tried to do here seemed to be wrong. And when they arrived at Silver Ridge, things seemed to get worse instead of better. Mrs. Fuller met them at the door with a martyred expression.

'So you've found the young lady?' she asked. 'I'm glad Miss Bartlett's back, for it's all I can do to watch the dinner without having to watch young boys as well. My health isn't up to it, Mr. Trent. I feel my migraine attack hasn't really gone yet, and the noise that Adrian makes when Damon plays with him doesn't help by any means.'

'Don't worry, Mrs. Fuller. I'm sure Taryn can give you a hand as soon as she's dried herself off.'

So, instead of the hot bath she had longed for, Taryn found that she had to make do with a brisk rub down with a towel and then go into the kitchen where Mrs. Fuller seemed to take a delight in making comments about the fact that she found her incompetent. Of course it is always difficult to work in a strange kitchen, especially when you are being supervised by someone who obviously wishes to think you are stupid. Taryn, who was usually neat and deft

34

at domestic things, found herself dropping things and being generally thoroughly clumsy. But at last the dinner had been served and the evening came to an end. The children were in bed and while she helped Adrian and tidied the bedrooms, she could hear a steady drone of conversation coming from the direction of the kitchen where Mrs. Fuller, in spite of the migraine, seemed to be holding forth to Ross.

What could she be saying? Taryn supposed she would soon know.

She descended rather timidly to the living-room and found that Ross was sitting on one of the leather chairs, his legs stretched towards the blaze of the log fire that had been lit earlier because of the chilly conditions outside. In the light of the flames, his expression seemed thoughtful and brooding. Only a brass lamp furnished a little extra light and the rest of the room was in shadow.

'Oh, Taryn, I'm glad you've come. I want to talk to you. Do sit down. No, not there. Come nearer where I can see you.'

Reluctantly she came to the seat he indicated where she was very near to him and had to regard him face to face in the firelight. They seemed to be together in a little island of soft golden light with the rest of the room in darkness. It gave too intimate an atmosphere to the conversation. His dark blue eyes looked almost black as he regarded her gravely.

'Taryn, I told you when I met you that you were not the type of person I'd expected. I had thought an older woman would be engaged, someone who could manage the children and give the extra help that would be needed in the house. I think you took this job impulsively without realizing what you were letting yourself in for, isn't that so?'

She started to stammer some kind of answer, but he interrupted her.

'Don't think that I'm not grateful. I'm glad someone could be found willing to undertake the journey at short notice. But I'm placed in an awkward position. Mrs. Fuller, who's been with me quite a while, seems to think you're too young and irresponsible to stay here.

35

'There's a lot of extra work involved in having three children in the house and I see now that perhaps I shouldn't have expected that she should cope with it. Perhaps it would be better if I employed a more competent African, though it's hard to get them to stay in these wild surroundings. They all want to go to the town.

'And of course I'm trying to engage a tutor who can help the children to get accustomed to the new syllabus they'll have to face at school in a couple of months' time.'

'You mean you want me to go?' asked Taryn.

'Not immediately. Of course I don't mean that. But I thought that I should warn you that I don't consider the present arrangement altogether satisfactory. I've always followed the rule in business that if someone doesn't seem suitable for any particular job it's best to face facts.'

'And get rid of them,' said Taryn rather bitterly.

She was disappointed. She had tried very hard to do her best in a job that was strange and bewildering, and now because Mrs. Fuller seemed to have taken a dislike to her she was to be asked to leave.

'What do you feel about staying? Do the children worry you?'

'Not in the least. I think I could become very fond of them. Of course Melinda wants her own way, but what young girl doesn't these days? And I love this countryside. I'm just a little puzzled to know what's expected of me. But I shall try my best to get on with your housekeeper. Perhaps the migraine was giving her a jaundiced view of me tonight.'

The frown on his face was replaced by a charming smile.

'Well, my dear, that's all I want to know. If you're not unhappy so far we can see how you settle down. A few weeks should make all the difference. I was hoping you could stay at least as long as the children are here. When they go to school, the circumstances will change. But you can be sure if you do have to leave I shall see that you get home safely or otherwise get another job here. Time will tell. And now I think you should go to bed. You've had a long day.'

He talks to me as if I were a child, thought Taryn. But she was relieved that she was to stay. However difficult the position, and there was no doubt it was difficult with a hostile Mrs. Fuller to deal with and a self-willed young girl like Melinda, she would hate to give up so soon. There was something about this mountain country that fascinated her. And Ross? Certainly he seemed a difficult man and a hard man to cross, but she would like to have his approval. Oh, yes, that was one thing that was certain.

CHAPTER THREE

TARYN had lain awake for some time in spite of the tiring day she had had with all its varying emotions. When she had been in bed for about an hour, she thought she heard the phone ring and Ross's voice speaking for what seemed quite a while. Once or twice she heard his laugh ringing out, then as quickly suppressed. So she was not unduly surprised when he came down to breakfast and announced that Coral was arriving that very morning. Someone had offered her a lift to the nearest small town, and Ross was to pick her up there.

'It will be a good opportunity to buy some better walking shoes for the three of you,' he informed the children. 'There's quite a decent shop there and we can get you all better shod than you are at present.'

Melinda, who had been toying with her oatmeal porridge, looked up, her face transformed by that lovely smile of hers. When it had been announced that Coral was arriving, she had looked sulky, but now at the promise of an expedition with Ross, her expression was radiant.

'Are you taking us too, Ross? Oh, super!'

They clattered off up the stairs to get ready for the trip and Taryn was left alone with Ross.

He smiled ruefully. 'They seem very pleased to have an expedition into town,' he commented.

'But children always enjoy something novel,' she assured him.

'I'm afraid you're going to be left behind. I thought perhaps if you were left alone for a while you could improve your acquaintance with Mrs. Fuller and perhaps give her some help in preparing for Coral's arrival. She'll have the gold room in my wing. She usually prefers that. Perhaps you could improve the look of the living-room and of course her room with some kind of flower arrangements. I know there are no garden flowers around, but you could do something with dry grass. Coral is quite clever at that kind of thing.'

If she likes doing the arrangements, won't she object to my taking it over? thought Taryn, but she did not say anything because she could hardly object to the first definite instruction she had had in this most vague and puzzling job.

When the children had departed with Ross, the house seemed very quiet except for the distant hum of a polisher where Moses was improving the already shining floors. Taryn employed herself tidying the children's rooms. She was uncertain what was to happen about the washing, so collected the soiled garments that had accumulated so far and, making a bundle of them, made her way rather reluctantly down to the kitchen.

Mrs. Fuller gave her a cold stare. She was sitting at the yellow-wood table in the centre of the room, drinking coffee and smoking a cigarette. When Taryn asked what arrangements she should make about the children's washing, Mrs. Fuller sighed wearily and, stubbing her cigarette, drained the dregs of her coffee as if to imply that Taryn had disturbed her few leisure moments of the day. She informed her that the laundry was an annexe of the kitchen and that there was a washing machine and a drying machine there. It seemed that this house, although it was in the country, had everything in the way of modern equipment. But then one would expect that from anything belonging to a person like Ross, Taryn thought.

She went into the laundry and gazed rather despondently at the gleaming equipment. She had not been used to such luxuries and hated to admit to Mrs. Fuller that she did not know how to work them. Then to her relief she saw there was a book of instructions hanging on a hook, so she seized this and found it all seemed simple enough. She set it working and everything went according to plan, so, feeling more satisfied with herself, she repaired to the kitchen and tried to win the approval of Mrs. Fuller by telling her that she had started the washing and was there anything else she could do to help in the kitchen in the meantime?

'I suppose someone will have to get the room ready for

Miss Swann,' Mrs. Fuller replied grudgingly. 'Very fussy and particular, Miss Swann is. It's "Mrs. Fuller, won't you be a dear, and press my dress," or "Mrs. Fuller, there seems to be a teeny spider's web in my room. Would you be a pet and get Moses to remove it?" Oh, yes, she's full of charm, Miss Swann is, but she likes her own way. I don't know what I'll do if they ever decide to make a match of it. Of course, there's one thing – they wouldn't spend much time here. Miss Swann likes living in town. I'm surprised she's coming today, specially with those children around.'

This was the longest speech Taryn had heard from Mrs. Fuller and, she thought, the most interesting. Reluctantly the housekeeper led the way to the linen room and handed out daffodil yellow sheets, directing her to a room that glowed with a light wood fourposter and a deep gold wallpaper.

'That's Mr. Trent's room just along the passage,' Mrs. Fuller told her. 'When you've fixed Miss Swann's room, perhaps you could see if it needs tidying. Moses is a bit careless and I don't fancy coming up again when it isn't necessary. After all, you are supposed to be here to do some work. Otherwise what did Mr. Trent pay your fare for?'

She stomped off before Taryn could reply. It was stupid to feel nettled when what Mrs. Fuller had said was perfectly true. The gold room with its luxurious carpeting of thick fur pile was spotlessly clean and the bed was soon made up. She would see about some kind of floral arrangement later. Rather timidly she made her way along the passage and opened the door into Ross's apartment.

Here the large room with its sloping thatched roof and heavy wooden beams was dominated by a huge bed. It must be very old, she thought, for the head and base were panelled with red Florentine leather in an intricate design of gilding, and the four posts were carved statues of gold angels. The walls were painted a plain white, but there was a triptych, three paintings in glowing reds and blues that filled the space above the stone fireplace. Taryn was surprised. Somehow she had expected something more austere, but of course Ross was a wealthy man, a man who could indulge his taste for luxury even in his country home.

There was no dressing table, but a red lacquered cabinet, although of Eastern origin, blended with the colours of the fantastic bed. Taryn went across to this and took up the heavy silver brushes that were a little awry. Although they shone brilliantly, she rubbed them with her duster, lingering over the beautiful pattern enclosing the initials R.T. Certainly there was no fault to find with how Mrs. Fuller and Moses kept this room. It was the main bedroom and evidently everything had to be perfect.

From the wide window, there was a glorious view of the long jagged range of blue peaks, and below in the valley, the river wound its white rippling way amongst the rocks. On the nearer slopes Taryn could see three huge antelopes grazing peacefully and she wondered what kind of antelope they could be. She felt she still had such a lot to learn about this country, for everything was strange.

Mrs. Fuller was having another cup of coffee when Taryn returned to the kitchen, but she did not offer her any. She smiled enigmatically and said, 'Just go and have a look at the laundry.'

Taryn did not like her expression and did not know what to expect. However, Moses had got there before her.

'Hau, missus,' he said. 'Plenty soap. Too much soap. Make mess.'

The previously immaculate laundry was awash with drifts of foam that had oozed through the top of the machine and deposited itself on the floor.

Mrs. Fuller stood in the doorway as Taryn rushed to help Moses.

'I thought you would have known that when you only put a few things in a washing machine you should lower the quantity of soap you use,' she said. 'Now Moses has got all this work when he should be cleaning the stove for me.'

'I'll do it,' said Taryn.

'Nonsense. Mr. Trent said you were to do light work and it's more than my job's worth to go against his wishes.'

Her expression seemed to say, 'It's nice to be some people,' but all she actually said was, 'He suggested you should do flower arrangements, so why don't you get on with it?'

'Where do you think I could find any suitable flowers?'

'If you walk around in this area you're bound to find something. Personally I think it's a lot of nonsense. Miss Swann fusses around with dry grass and wild flowers, but she doesn't have to clear up the mess that they make when they drop so easily. She just picks things around here, bits of twigs and grasses. I must say she does know what she's doing.'

'Is there anything else that you need help with?'

'Not that I could trust you to do. They won't be back until late afternoon, so after lunch I'll be able to put my feet up. There are biscuits and cheese there if you need to take something with you.'

It was a long time since they had had breakfast and Taryn's appetite had increased in the fresh mountain air. She helped herself to the biscuits and cheese, wishing she had been offered the alternative of making a few sandwiches for herself. Obviously Mrs. Fuller was eager to get rid of her. As she walked away from the house, she saw her settling down upon the verandah in a kind of chaise-longue with a well laden tray upon the table beside her.

She had thought of walking to the trout hatchery, for surely Mrs. Schroeder would be able to spare her some flowers from the garden, but then she thought that Ross might not like her to ask for them. She was obviously expected to display some initiative. Mrs. Fuller had said that Coral made beautiful arrangements from dry grass and twigs. However did you do that?

She took a path in the opposite direction to the one she had traversed yesterday afternoon. It led along the face of the mountain, but along its grassy lower slopes, only a track, but not difficult because it was fairly level. All the time she kept looking around at the vegetation. The grasses looked very lovely where they were growing, but she could not imagine them arranged in a vase. Her life in London had been too busy, too full of tasks that had to be done to take any interest in a subject like flower arrangement.

42

She wandered on, not finding the object of her search, but enjoying the sunshine, the clear vibrant air, the vast landscape of hills and mountains all around her, green on the lower slopes, then fading into softest blue in the distance. She came to a small gate and decided to sit on a kind of stile and eat an apple before going further. A peacock butterfly came to settle on the peel, lazily flapping its wings in the heat of the sun. As she walked on she noticed beetles frantically pushing quite large balls of the material they had scavenged. It was amusing to watch their frenzied efforts. First they would perch upon their prize, then another beetle would get upon it and so tip the balance and the ball would roll down the slope. Taryn wished the children were with her or someone else to share the laughter she felt bubbling up inside her at the sight of the insect's queer antics.

Thinking this, she began to feel a bit lonely. It was odd, after being used to living in a big city, to find herself transported to this vast landscape where the only living things beside herself were that soaring black eagle high above the crag, three antelope moving across the slopes, and a honey bird sipping nectar from the large pink flowers some way up the hill. She stopped dead. Flowers? Oh, yes, they looked very suitable and would be easy to arrange, she felt sure.

She had a knife with her, the one with which she had peeled the apple. Just a few branches would make a good arrangement in the living-room and she would try to find something smaller for Coral's bedroom. Having cut them and feeling pleased with herself now, she strolled on, trying to decide which of the small flowers that dotted the grass would last if picked.

The antelope must have noticed her, for they were moving swiftly further up the hill. But no, it wasn't she who had disturbed them, but a figure on a horse, riding towards her along the trail, still a long way off but rapidly approaching.

As he drew near Taryn saw upon the sturdy mountain pony a young man whose bright red hair glinted in the sun. When he had come to a halt and dismounted, she found he was of middle height, taller than herself but by no means as

tall or broad as Ross, but all the same a strong, sturdy looking man in some kind of uniform, a large hat upturned at one
side. His skin, though brown and ruddy, was freckled, and
he regarded her with keen, bright blue eyes. It would have
been a pleasant face, but at the moment was marred by a
frown.

'What the hell do you think you're doing?' he asked. 'I
couldn't believe my eyes when I saw you through my binoculars picking those proteas. Don't you know all the
flowers in the reserve are protected? Or didn't you read the
notice you were given when you came to your hutted
camp?'

Taryn was taken aback and stared at the angry young
man, quite unable to defend herself.

'There seems to be no end to people's vandalism! Only
the other day I came across some young boys painting their
names on to a rock with whitewash, and now here are you,
who look a perfectly well brought up schoolgirl, with an
armful of proteas that you have no right to at all!'

'I'm not a schoolgirl,' said Taryn, stung to protest. 'I'm
twenty years old.'

'Then you should know better.'

'How was I to know that your wretched flowers were protected?'

'For crying out loud! You got a list of regulations as soon
as you entered the reserve at the lower gate. The African
guard hands them out. But I suppose you were just too lazy
to read them.

'I didn't enter by the lower gate. I came over that stile.
And I'm not at the hutted camp, whatever that might be. I
came over the hill from Silver Ridge.'

The young man looked surprised.

'Oh, so you're staying at Ross Trent's place? Are you a
relative?'

'No,' said Taryn, but gave no explanation.

'I heard he had some young relatives coming to stay there.
I hope you all behave yourselves a bit better than the last
people who stayed there. Ross is all right, but I can't say as
much for some of his friends. The last lot started a fire on

44

the mountain with their cigarette butts when they went for a moonlight bathe in the stream. Not to speak of the way they disturbed the animals around there.'

'I'm looking after the three children and I can assure you they don't smoke,' Taryn told him. 'But if you give me a copy of these regulations, I'll try to see that they keep them. No one told me this was a reserve, but I've only just come from England.'

The young man's manner had relaxed and he even started to smile. He had a good-natured face really, thought Taryn. And after all, she supposed he had been fierce because it was his job to look after the place.

'You seem to have plenty of excuses. Well, this time you won't get fined. If you haven't seen the camp and you have time I'll take you there and get you a copy of the rules. It's just along the path over that little hill.'

He led the horse and walked beside Taryn.

'I'm Mike Murray, by the way. You might as well call me Mike. Everyone does.'

Taryn told him her name. She was eager to make amends. It had been a bad mistake, she supposed, to pick the flowers. But how was she to know it was forbidden? She would not have dreamed of picking flowers in a London park, but it seemed odd in this place, that had miles and miles of apparently lonely and untouched country, that one should not be able to please oneself. However, she supposed these rules were necessary.

Around a turn of the path, nestling upon the hillside, were the group of small houses that comprised what Mike had called 'the hutted camp'. They were small square thatched huts, quite basic, but with a beautiful view of the whole range of blue mountains. Mike said people came to stay here, bringing their own food that was prepared by African staff in central kitchens. One of the huts a little apart from the rest was the office, and nearby Mike pointed to his house. When he was giving her the list of rules he had promised, a black servant in a white overall came in and spoke to him. He had a tray and towel in his hand and was presumably calling Mike to a meal.

45

'Thank you very much,' Taryn said hastily. 'I'm sorry about the proteas. Can I give them back to you now, because I think I should be on my way. I don't want to interrupt your lunch.'

'No, no, stay a while. You may as well keep the proteas. They're no use to me now. Where are you going to eat?'

When she confessed that she was going to lunch on cheese and biscuits, he pressed her to eat with him.

'Ambrose always prepares enough for half a dozen. And afterwards I can run you back to Silver Ridge in the truck. I have some business over that way.'

Taryn, thinking of the long lonely afternoon ahead of her with only a sulky Mrs. Fuller for company, accepted the invitation and they went over to Mike's house where they ate a simple but adequate meal of shepherd's pie and tinned peas.

'Do you live here alone?' Taryn asked, glancing around at the neat but very basic living-room with its couple of cane chairs and deal table.

'It looks like it, doesn't it?' grinned Mike, who had seen her inspection of the room. 'Not much feminine touch, is there?'

'I like it,' said Taryn. 'You hardly need feminine touches when you have such a glorious view.'

'It gets a bit lonely sometimes, but I'm used to it and there's always plenty to do. The superintendent of the camp is away for a few days and I'm doing his work. My own work is more in connection with looking after the reserve and the things that grow there. You know from experience I haven't much patience with visitors. I feel they are a bit superfluous. What matters is keeping the reserve in a natural state and fighting off any threat to change it.'

'Do any women live here permanently?' asked Taryn.

'The superintendent has a wife who helps him with the camp. It's risky to bring a girl to this kind of life. It takes a special kind of person to enjoy the wilds, even if it's as lovely as this. Most girls these days prefer the material things of life, and want beautiful furniture and everything that opens and shuts to make life easy. In a place like this

46

you have to learn to amuse yourself and not to get bored easily.'

'Ross Trent seems to prefer the life there. He doesn't seem to find it boring.'

Mike laughed a bit ironically.

'Ross Trent? The trout hatcheries are just a rich man's hobby. And if any girl-friend of his became bored with the mountain scenery, he could easily whisk her off to town. Not everyone can afford dinners at swank hotels.'

Taryn wondered if Mike sounded bitter. Perhaps he had been turned down by some girl-friend who would not venture to share his life as a ranger. But as they rode back in the truck with Taryn clutching the forbidden bunch of proteas and a few geraniums and yellow daisies Mike had given her from the small patch of garden in front of the absent superintendent's house, he sounded more cheerful, pointing out the sights that she herself might have missed, a tortoise crossing the road, a leguan, a large two-foot lizard, sitting at the door of its hole and catching insects in the sunlight.

'Are you staying here long?' he asked, as they came near to the house. 'Perhaps I shall see you again?'

'I don't know,' she replied. 'It depends upon how long Ross Trent needs me to see to the children. I took this job in a hurry and it's all a bit vague.'

'Do you really mean it when you say you like it here and would like to stay?'

'Well,' Taryn replied cautiously, 'so far I think it's wonderful, but I've only been here since yesterday. I only know that I want to see more of it. I hope I do have to stay for a while. I must go now. I must arrange these flowers, and Mrs. Fuller may need some help before the family arrives back.'

He got out of the truck to help her down from the high cab and he was holding her hands just as the silver Mercedes swung to a halt beside them. Coral leaned out of the passenger seat, looking quite beautiful in a sleeveless white slacks suit that flattered her even golden tan and her dark hair.

'Hello, Taryn, what have you been up to?'

The remark was supposed to be good-natured, but Taryn

47

thought she detected an undercurrent of sarcasm and wished she had managed to arrive home before Ross and the children, because it really looked as if she had been neglecting her duties. But she was soon surrounded by the three children all wanting to tell her about their day in town, and with a wave of his hand, Mike got back into the truck, calling as he drove away, 'I'll see you again, Taryn!'

'You are a quick worker, Taryn. You surprise me,' said Coral. 'And how did you persuade Mike to give you those gorgeous proteas? Ross has always told me it's more than my life's worth to pick any. You must have got on very friendly terms with Mike very quickly.'

Taryn did not reply. She stole a glance to see how Ross was reacting to Coral's observations. The dark blue eyes were looking at her as if they could drill into her thoughts and know the truth. But she was determined not to tell the little group of her blunder over cutting the precious flowers.

'Do let me arrange them,' pleaded Coral in a very charming manner. 'I'd simply love to, and I'm sure you can find plenty to do now the children have arrived back.'

'Would you ask Mrs. Fuller to bring some tea, Taryn?' asked Ross.

'And while you're going to the kitchen, you might as well fill this lovely copper jug with water for me,' put in Coral. 'Oh, and bring a newspaper and some clippers. I'll arrange them in here. I've seen so little of you today, Ross darling. Couldn't Taryn give tea to the children on the side verandah and we'll have it in here. There's so much I want to talk about.'

'Of course she always makes extra work. That means two trays,' Mrs. Fuller grumbled.

'I'll do them,' Taryn offered, but there was such an array of cups in the pantry that she had to ask which ones to use. Mrs. Fuller clicked her tongue and muttered under her breath that she might as well have done it herself.

It seemed that everyone's day had been spoiled by having to cater to Coral's whim. Melinda, who had been glowing with good spirits on her return, sat on a swinging seat and

48

sulkily accepted the tea that Taryn handed to her, together with one of the special little pastries they had brought from town.

'I thought we were going to have tea with Ross,' she grumbled. 'We bought these specially. Do you think she's going to turn us out every time she wants to be alone with him?'

'Sure to,' said Damon, grinning at her, and Taryn thought he had some of Ross's teasing quality. 'We might as well put camp beds on the verandah, don't you think so, Taryn?'

'You've been with Ross all day, so there's no need to sulk, Melinda. Naturally Coral wants to be alone with Ross sometimes.'

'Why are you fussing, Melinda?' asked Adrian. 'It's nice here without Coral. May I have another cake, Taryn?'

After they had finished tea, Taryn carried the tray back into the kitchen. Mrs. Fuller was not there and she could hear the sounds of the guitar that Moses played in his room outside. She washed up the cups and wondered whether she should go to collect the other tray. Suddenly the voice of Ross rang out loud and clear in the kitchen. But where was he, and surely he could not have mistaken Taryn for the plump figure of the housekeeper, for he had said, 'Mrs. Fuller, will you send Moses to collect the debris?' She then realized that the voice had come from a small shelf where the intercom stood, but she had no idea how to work it, so, taking a dustpan and broom that she saw handy, she made her way to the living-room.

'Oh, it's you,' said Coral.

She was sitting on the rug in front of the settee, her head against Ross's knee. They had put a match to the fire, and the flames from the logs flickered upon her lovely face. It was a very intimate scene and after a moment's pause to indicate to Taryn that she should clear up the leaves and twigs left over from the flower arranging, Coral went on talking to Ross as if they were alone in the room.

'You don't seem to realize, Ross, that there's absolutely no need for you to stay with these children. Surely Mrs.

49

Fuller and Taryn here can cope with them. What do you pay people for?'

'I prefer to stay for a while until they've settled down. I shall come to town occasionally. My business manager is quite able to do his work and I can get there very easily if he needs me. That's what I pay him for.'

There was an ironical note in Ross's voice and Coral seemed to decide to adopt different tactics. She rose and slid down on to the settee next to him, twining her arm in his.

'I miss you so much. Do come back. Town isn't the same without you.'

'You can always come here – you know that.'

'I have come, and you should appreciate it. But I don't want to spend much time here, nor do you. You know you really like city life. This craze about the mountains and wild life is simply a phase. You never used to be like this.'

Ross sounded displeased.

'I had hoped you would want to get to know the children better, but if you find it dull, you know what to do.'

He smiled lazily and Taryn had a fleeting feeling of being sorry for Coral. With her beauty, she must surely be used to having her own way with men, but Ross seemed to be a tough proposition. He was a man who was willing to take what he wanted from a woman without being influenced by her desires in the least.

'I don't intend to leave until you're willing to come with me. In any case, I haven't got a car here. You'll have to take me back to Durban.'

'Don't be too sure. There's a luxury bus that leaves twice a week from the nearest town. You could always take that.'

Coral got up and strode with her long mannequin walk towards the door.

'You're quite infuriating! I'm going to change for dinner and you can mix me a very dry Martini to make up for your obstinacy.'

She almost banged the door as she shut it. Ross got up and flung another log on to the fire so that a flurry of sparks fled up the chimney. Then he turned to Taryn, who was wondering how she could appear invisible.

'So, Taryn, and are you as bored as Coral with this dull countryside and all these monotonous mountains?'

'I . . . I . . .' What could she say? It would sound so priggish if she said she was loving it. Especially after Coral's manifest dislike of the situation.

'You're being paid to stay here, of course, so you don't have much choice.'

How insufferable he could be! If he hoped to vent his irritation on her he had come to the wrong person.

'I've never hesitated to leave any job that I found distasteful or monotonous, Mr. Trent. If I find this job not to my liking, I won't hesitate to leave, even if I am a stranger in a strange country.'

And you can chew that over, Ross, with your dark blue eyes looking at me as if that bronze antelope on the shelf had suddenly come to life and started to answer back.

But he threw back his head and laughed, and Taryn found this even more exasperating.

'You may look like a rather quiet schoolgirl, but I see you have quite a few surprises in store. And tell me, how did you persuade Mike to give you those proteas?'

There was a wicked gleam in his expression. Oh, why did he have to ask about the proteas when she had been trying to put him down a little?

'It was a mistake,' she confessed, and then indignantly, 'Why did no one explain to me that it was a reserve? You told me to pick flowers for an arrangement.'

'I admit it. But you may remember I spoke about dry grasses and thought you would find them near to the house. I didn't expect you would wander so far afield. I would have admitted my responsibility and paid your fine for you. But you seem to have charmed Mike. He didn't look too furious when he delivered you here.'

'I liked him,' said Taryn.

'So.' The blue eyes considered her. 'Yes, he's a good chap. He had a girl-friend who ran out on him when she also decided that this part of the world was boring. How you women seem to long for the city! Mike will take quite a lot of catching another time, I warn you.'

'He's not a trout, and anyhow I'm not fishing,' said Taryn, 'and now if you'll excuse me, I'd better take this away and see if I can give Mrs. Fuller any help.'

CHAPTER FOUR

'YOU can take Miss Swann's tray up to her room,' said Mrs. Fuller next morning, looking rather distastefully at Adrian, who was sitting at the kitchen table dribbling milk over his cornflakes with rather a lot of splashing. Taryn had decided that it would save the housekeeper some trouble if she fed the children and herself in the kitchen this morning. She had not realized that Coral would insist on having her breakfast in bed, but she might have known. She would get her own breakfast later. Already Coral's voice had sounded rather impatiently through the intercom.

'Mrs. Fuller, darling, do send my breakfast up soon. I know you're frightfully busy with all the children underfoot, but you know I only need a glass of orange juice and a lightly boiled egg and some very thin toast – and some of your delicious coffee, black of course.'

Taryn did her best to fulfil this order quickly while persuading Adrian to eat his bacon and egg. He had cut the white away, saying he didn't like it, and was busy dipping toast fingers into the runny yolk.

'I don't like to see children playing with their food,' said Mrs. Fuller.

Neither did Taryn, but she was keen that the little boy should eat. He had a poor appetite.

'Miss Swann likes the Paragon china. There's a breakfast set with gold roses in the pantry.'

It was amazing. There seemed to be a matching breakfast set for each guest room. Taryn took the fragile cups and plates and arranged them on a lacy traycloth. Coral was sitting up in bed, her hair a shining fall of darkness against the primrose pillows. She was wearing a flame-coloured nightdress with deeply plunging neckline, but implored Taryn to find her a bedjacket. She and Melinda were a pair, thought Taryn, as she turned over the jumble of fine underclothes in the suitcase and found the required garment, one of thinnest gossamerlike cashmere.

'Be a pet, Taryn, while you're here you might as well fold things and put them in the drawers. I didn't have time yesterday.'

Taryn did not much like playing lady's maid to Coral, but thought she had better do it with good grace. Coral evidently thought she had better use her charm, for afterwards she patted the bed and said, 'Do come and sit here. I hate to eat alone.'

Then why hadn't she gone down to have breakfast with Ross? Taryn wondered.

'I like to get up slowly. I'm never at my best in the morning. Don't you find that?'

Taryn had never had the opportunity to stay in bed for breakfast, so she made a noncommittal reply.

'It's most frightfully noble of Ross to have taken over these children, isn't it? But it means I can see so little of him. I should like some opportunity to see him alone, and I know he would. He can't really like having the children tagging along all the time. I was quite amazed when I found he'd brought them with him yesterday. It seems he's a bit surprised because you're so young and doesn't feel he can leave them with you.'

'I'm quite responsible,' said Taryn a little indignantly. What had Ross been saying to Coral? 'There's no reason why the children shouldn't be left with me. In fact that's what I'm here for.'

'That's exactly what I told Ross. Oh, Taryn dear, it's so hard when Ross and I are . . . well . . . almost engaged, never to be alone together. Couldn't you help me and reassure him that they'll be perfectly all right with you if he takes me out to lunch at the Mountain Inn? It isn't as if we'd be away for very long.'

Coral's lovely face was alive with pleading charm. No wonder Ross was in love with her. Taryn remembered that she had felt sorry for Coral last night when Ross had appeared so obstinate, and she reflected that it would be terrible to be in love with such a hard man. But doubtless Coral with her stunning physical attraction and her sophistication could cope with their life together.

'Please back me up,' Coral was saying. 'I can't stay here very long. I have to go back to my modelling assignments quite soon. Say you'll take them out for a picnic.'

When Taryn returned to the kitchen, Mrs. Fuller turned to her, saying, 'You take your time, I must say. Mr. Trent has been creating like fury because no one is there to eat with him. He says if you haven't had breakfast yet you'd better join him.'

Another person who did not like to eat alone! Taryn left Adrian playing with his cars and went into the dining-room. Ross was sitting at the head of the heavy mahogany table that could seat about twenty. Unlike Coral, he evidently did not take a long time to become lively, for his eyes were bright and every action seemed to tell of huge vitality.

'Oh, good morning, Taryn. I thought this house was full of people and yet there's no one at the breakfast table. Bring a slice of bread to this toaster, help yourself to an egg if you want one and sit down. No, not over there. Here next to me. Do you expect me to shout right down the length of the table, or don't you speak so early in the morning?'

He took up a silver instrument, nearly sliced off the top of a boiled egg, buttered a piece of toast and crunched it between his strong white teeth. This morning he looked very good-humoured, not a bit like the moody man who had flung the log on the fire after he had had words with Coral.

'Well, what's the programme for today? Coral will probably be a spot restless. The country has that effect on her. She had some proposition last night about going to lunch at the Mountain Inn. How would that suit you and the children?'

Taryn thought how horrified Coral would be if she knew that Ross intended to take them all.

'The children had an outing with you yesterday,' she said. 'Isn't it my turn to take them out? After all, I'm here to look after them, and really I'm quite responsible, even if you do think I look young. Let me take them for a picnic today. It will get them out of Mrs. Fuller's way and it will give you a chance to be with Coral.'

He looked at her quizzically. Really, no man had any right to be so handsome and dynamic first thing in the morning!

'If you girls are on first name terms already, what's wrong with calling me Ross? So you think I need to make my peace with Coral after last night? Well, perhaps you're right. The poor girl made the effort to come all the way here to visit me and the children. It's the least I can do to take her out to lunch.'

'You amaze me,' said Taryn. 'Any man in his right mind would be thrilled to be seen with such a beautiful girl and to have the chance of spending the day with her. But of course you must realize that.'

Surely even Ross could not be so conceited as to think that the good fortune was all on Coral's side in being taken to lunch by him.

'Yes, I must agree with you this time. Any man likes to be seen with the most beautiful girl in the room, and Coral certainly knows how to look both lovely and charming. She likes her own way, as you may have noticed, but most women can be tamed, I find.'

Was he trying to provoke her? His smile was mischievous as if he were teasing. He got up from the table.

'So be it. It's your decision. I shall take Coral to lunch, and if you feel capable you can help the children unpack the school books we brought yesterday and sort them out. I'm hoping I shall soon hear from the man who's coming to give them coaching. Then later, as you suggested, you might take them for a picnic. But keep to the paths and don't go wandering too far up the mountains. If you keep on the level there's no danger. Take a stick with you in case of snakes, but most of them will get away before you even see them. As you say, Taryn, I must trust you to be responsible, even if, with those huge brown eyes looking at me, you seem about twelve years old.'

Coral came down in a beautiful dress of green linen that exactly matched her eyes. Now that she had got her own way she was very charming and even thanked Taryn for furthering the plan. But Melinda was sulky.

'I wish Coral would go back to Durban,' she said. 'Ross promised he would take me riding and so far he hasn't said a word about it. Coral is trying to take up all his time.'

'But she isn't here for very long, and after all, she is . . .' Taryn almost said Ross's fiancée, but thought better of it . . . 'Ross's girl-friend,' she ended rather weakly.

'How do you know?' Melinda tossed her golden mane and her blue eyes flashed. 'I think she's just making a play for Ross. He can't really mean to marry her. He needs someone much nicer than her.'

'You don't even know her, Melinda. Let's go and unpack those books.'

'What a bore it is having to go to school again. And it will all be different.'

'Yes, well, that's why Ross is engaging this young tutor to coach you, so you won't have any trouble with the syllabus.'

'I hope he's good-looking,' said Melinda. 'If he is we might even get Coral to fall in love with him. Oh, I do wish we could get rid of Coral! I was so looking forward to meeting Ross again now I'm nearly grown-up, and that woman spoils everything.'

'Be careful with those books,' warned Taryn, for Melinda was hitting them together as if she had Coral between them. 'Stack them neatly in order. Don't jumble them up.'

'Oh, don't you start getting oldmaidish, Taryn! I do hope this tutor livens things up a bit. We haven't had much fun yet, with Coral monopolizing Ross all the time. I wonder what we could do to make her leave.'

Melinda's angelic face had an expression of deep concentration. Damon, who had been scarcely listening to the conversation up to now, looked at her with interest.

'Whenever Melly looks like that, something happens,' he told Taryn. 'Melly likes to get her own way.'

And so does Coral, thought Taryn.

When the books had been sorted, it was mid-morning and she went into the kitchen to consult Mrs. Fuller, who was sitting at the table with her inevitable cigarette and cup of coffee but had not offered them any refreshment.

'I intend to take the children out to lunch, Mrs. Fuller, I shall cut some sandwiches and pack a haversack. Can you suggest where we should go?'

'Let me think. You need a nice long walk if you intend to stay out for lunch, don't you?'

'Yes, I suppose so, but not too difficult for Adrian. Mr. Trent said we should stick to the paths and not do any climbing.'

'In that case I would say it might be a good idea to try the gorge path. It seems clear today. It gets a bit muddy if it rains.'

'What path is that?'

'It leads into a gorge where the river runs out from the mountain. There are some pretty waterfalls. Mind you, I haven't been there since I was much younger, but it's a very popular walk. During the holidays you can hardly get along the path for visitors.'

'It sounds all right. It won't be too difficult for Adrian?'

'Oh, no, it's perfectly straightforward. You go through some forest, but you can't miss the path. There's only one.'

Mrs. Fuller sounded quite amiable. She must be looking forward to a peaceful day. After all, it must have been a shock to her system to be landed with a whole household of people including three children when she usually had a very leisurely time. Perhaps she was getting used to them now, thought Taryn hopefully.

At any rate she was quite generous about producing cold beef to make sandwiches, slices of cake, a few apples and some cool drinks in a plastic bottle, and she pointed out the path that they must follow, winding down into the valley, then across the stream by a small wooden bridge and onwards until it disappeared around a curve of the hill.

'You're sure it won't be too far for Adrian?' asked Taryn.

'Well, you can always turn back if it is,' said Mrs. Fuller impatiently. 'I don't believe in mollycoddling children, especially boys. If he's going to spend any time here he must

58

get used to walking. I'm sure that's what Mr. Trent would say.'

It was a beautiful day for walking. Even Melinda, who had not been too keen to come, stopped looking bored after a while. The sun was shining and they needed the hats they had brought, but the breeze was cool and tempered the heat. When they reached the stream, they paused on the bridge watching the clear pewter-coloured water bubbling over the little stones and sweeping past the green plants that grew on either side.

Damon was inclined to show off, using the bridge like parallel bars in a gymnasium and swinging rather precariously backwards and forwards, then turning a somersault. Melinda regarded his behaviour with the scorn of a more mature fifteen to a boyish thirteen, but Taryn had hard work to dissuade Adrian from trying this too.

At length they started off again, along the path which ascended until they were walking above the winding river. On either side was grassland sloping upwards to the lower curves of the hills and the pathway was clearly defined. It seemed a simple enough walk, thought Taryn. Suddenly there was a harsh bark that sounded very near. The children stopped and looked questioningly at Taryn, who was trying hard to conceal the fact that the odd noise had startled her. It came again . . . 'Bom . . . bom', a defiant warning note.

'There they are!' shouted Adrian. 'Big monkeys!'

Half a dozen black forms were leaping like hobgoblins, running with queer bobbing steps up the hillside but pausing every now and again to look back and shout.

'They're not ordinary monkeys,' said Damon. 'They're baboons. Do you remember them in the zoo, Melinda?'

'Oh, yes, they were hideous,' said Melinda, shuddering. 'Do let's go on, Taryn. I can't bear to see them.'

'They seem to be just as frightened of us,' Taryn reassured her. She did not say that behind them she had seen a huge one sitting on a rock not many yards away. It must be the guard, posted as a lookout to warn the pack when danger was near. She was glad when they came to a turn of the path, where they found themselves walking amongst old tangled

59

trees, that looked as if they had been there for hundreds of years. The sweet fragrance of wild jasmine was wafted towards them together with the sound of the stream that seemed wider now, rushing along its course between great rocks down below.

The boys had run on ahead and Melinda was wandering along dreamily in some private thoughts of her own. Taryn thought how fortunate she had been, in spite of all the little niggling worries, to be sent to this lovely part of the world. True, Mrs. Fuller was a bit hard to tolerate, but how could one expect everything to be perfect? And Ross? She was not very sure what she thought of him. She had never before met a man of his type, sure and confident in the possession of a strong personality. Did that come from the fact that he was so wealthy? But no, if he had been a game ranger like Mike she could imagine that he would be just as certain of himself.

She thought of the other two, Ross and Coral, making their way up to the Mountain Inn. What would it be like, she wondered, to be beautiful and exquisitely dressed like Coral and to be going up through wonderful mountain scenery to have lunch with a man who was in love with you? She knew the inn was high up on the pass on a new road that made travelling easy for driving through this wild country. But the road would be lonely at this time when it was not the holiday season, so they would encounter little traffic. Would Ross drive slowly, turning every now and again to look at Coral's pure profile and hold those long slender fingers? She surprised in herself a twinge of envy and then felt guilty for this, when she should be enjoying their pleasant walk. How would you like to be back in London in pouring rain and cold weather? she admonished herself.

Damon and Adrian came running back along the path.

'It gets exciting further on. There are a lot of rocks where the river goes through.'

She looked at Adrian's flushed face.

'Are you sure you're all right, Adrian? You aren't tired?'

But he shrugged off her anxiety and declared sturdily, 'I want to go further. There's a kind of tunnel where the river goes through to the other side of the rocks.'

They turned a corner of the path, then they were through a little wood and down to the river which was now a broad stretch of water running between huge boulders. On either side, cliffs enclosed the water and further on was the opening of a kind of tunnel, but it was really a gorge formed by the rocks coming close together and almost meeting at the top. High above them, but seeming much nearer than they actually were, the blue mountains towered in rugged peaks.

The going was more difficult now, and Taryn wondered how Mrs. Fuller could have described this as an easy walk, but the children were keen to get to the tunnel and even Adrian would not hear of turning back. They found they had to boulder-hop from one side of the stream to the other, carefully picking stepping stones. They took off their shoes and socks, and it was just as well, for occasionally the stone upturned and they found themselves with their feet in the water, but it was shallow and they came to no harm. By the entrance of the tunnel, they came to a halt. The river ran on through the gloom and seemed to look much deeper. Taryn firmly called a halt.

'We can go no further,' she said. 'It looks far too dangerous. Let's sit down and have lunch and then we shall start back.'

Damon was the first to finish and started wandering around inspecting the place. Suddenly he gave a shout, 'Look here, there's a chain ladder that goes up the cliff. It must lead to a route on top of the tunnel and gets you to the other side. I'm going to try it.'

'No, don't do that, Damon,' said Taryn. 'I'd hate you to climb it on your own, and Adrian certainly can't attempt it.'

'Of course I can do it,' Damon declared defiantly. 'I do far worse things than that in P.T. It won't take me long. I promise I'll be careful.'

'Let him go,' urged Melinda: 'He's quite capable of

climbing that little ladder. Why do you always think you have to play nursemaid to us? Adrian is the only one who really needs you.'

'I'm not,' said Adrian, offended. 'I could climb that ladder if I wanted to, but I don't.'

'Very well,' said Taryn. I suppose it's silly to be nervous about them, she thought. Certainly Ross would want them to be independent and fearless. And I suppose the ladder must be safe. It's put there for people to save the scramble up the cliff.

'Let me go with Damon and you stay with Adrian,' Melinda suggested.

'No, I'd prefer to go myself and let you stay with Adrian,' Taryn answered.

'Oh, all right,' Melinda replied a bit ungraciously. 'Ooh, look!' They all gazed at a large blueheaded lizard that had darted out on to the rock beside the one upon which they were sitting. 'Isn't it hideous?' asked Melinda delightedly.

'It's beautiful,' said Adrian, staring solemnly as the weird creature rushed around catching large ants. Taryn was glad he was pleased, that he did not seem particularly interested in trying to climb the ladder. She was rather tired herself and wished Damon was not so enthusiastic, but she would simply hate to let him disappear over the top and not know what was happening.

The steel ladder was fixed with staples against the face of the cliff, but the rock had been curved by the force of water and was smooth and rather slippery to the feet and hands. But if you progressed steadily and did not look down, it was not so bad. Taryn tried not to think of the distance that was growing ever greater as they made their slow way to the top. Finally she heaved herself over on to the grass verge and looked around. A narrow path led through overhanging bushes along the cliff edge.

'This must lead to the tunnel eventually,' said Damon.

But it was hard to see where it led because the path was almost overgrown and there was grass as high as their heads on either side. All at once the path began to descend.

'Hold on,' said Damon, who had insisted on leading the way. 'This looks like fun. We have to do some climbing here. There are pitons in the rock for your feet.'

There was a narrow place between two smooth rocks and where the footholds were scarce iron spikes had been placed to make the descent possible.

'Let me go first,' Taryn insisted.

She had the gravest doubts about this whole adventure by now, but there was no going back. It would be impossible to climb down the steel ladder. They could only go forward. She climbed doggedly down the narrow crevice, reaching out with her feet and then watching Damon who was following closely so that she could advise him where to stand. At last, to her great relief, they were down with no mishap and another grassy path led to the end of the tunnel. At the back of them the blue mountains soared up with one grand narrow needle of a peak commanding the landscape.

But now they met a snag. They found themselves up on top of a high rock above the pool and the entrance to the tunnel was on the other side of this across a deep stretch of water. Over a huge boulder that was slimy with wet green moss hung another steel ladder. It was not, however, easily negotiable like the first one, but hung horizontally against the rock so that the only way to get across was to slide one's feet along the side of the rung.

'Isn't it exciting?' asked Damon. 'It's just like a commando course.'

Too much so, thought Taryn. It seemed quite impossible to her to negotiate the passage across the rock to the other side above the deep dark pool, and yet it had to be done.

'I'll go first this time,' said Damon, and without further ado he was off.

'Take it slowly,' Taryn implored him, but he was being fairly cautious, sliding his feet across the metal and clasping hold of the rock beyond it. Towards the middle the ladder began to sway, but Damon was more amused than scared.

'It's just like that flick, *The Poseidon Adventure*,' he shouted. 'Come on, Taryn, I'll give you a hand when you get to this end.'

With an immense effort of will, she left the firm ground and put her feet upon the first part of the horizontal ladder. Sliding one foot across, she found she had to lift it to put it beyond the rung. She knew now what it must feel like when climbing to have to force yourself to go on and to cling like a spider to the rock face. With intense effort she managed to get to the middle. But here the ladder began to sway. Although light she was heavier than Damon, of course, and the pitons supporting the ladder had been loosened by the rushing water during storms.

'Give me your hand,' she heard Damon shout, but he was too far away and, before she could save herself, the ladder swung over and deposited her into the water below. She felt stunned, but managed to swim to the rock where Damon was standing, although she was conscious of a tearing pain in her left ankle. Damon helped her to the dry rock. His face was white and scared.

'Gee, Taryn, are you all right? I never thought the ladder would up-end like that.'

She tried to smile, but a wave of faintness made her bend forwards.

'Don't worry, Damon, I'll be all right in a minute. It's just that I seem to have hurt my ankle when I fell. What a nuisance! Well, fortunately I've got the stick with me. We'll have to try to hobble along. I'm afraid it's going to slow us up.'

Afterwards she could not remember how she got through the tunnel. The distance was not far, but the river ran between the walls of high cliffs and there were rocks to negotiate. But now it did not matter about getting wet, for she was soaked to the skin anyway. When they came near to the end, she heard Damon, who had gone ahead, calling to Melinda, and they both came back and held on to her elbows as they emerged in to the sunlight again. So far sheer determination had carried her through this ordeal, but now she took off her walking boot and sock and found that already her ankle was swelling rapidly.

'It can't be broken,' she said. 'More like a bad sprain. But we'd better start for home before it gets any worse.'

However, when she tried to stand again, she was forced to the conclusion that it was hopeless.

'Melinda, I'm dreadfully sorry, I really don't think I can walk. Will you three make your way home and ask for help? I don't think Ross will have returned yet, so you'd better phone one of the rangers. You could ask for Mike Murray. Whoever comes could bring a horse or mule. I think I could manage to ride.'

'I'm staying with you,' said Damon. 'Ross wouldn't want me to leave you. Besides, it was partly my fault.'

'I can't go alone,' said Melinda. Her lips quivered and she looked like a little girl.

'Why not?' demanded Damon. 'You'll have Adrian for company.'

'The baboons,' said Melinda. 'I can't face going past that place where the baboons were. They were so big and frightening. If one shouted at me like they did before, I think I should faint if I were alone with Adrian.'

'You go too, Damon,' said Taryn hastily. 'It's good of you to want to stay, but I shall be quite all right and it will be of much more use if you go with Melinda and Adrian. It won't take very long really and no harm can come to me here. I'll be much happier if I know you're all on your way home.'

She watched the figures of the three children become smaller and smaller as they made their way down the gorge. Where the path led into the trees they turned and waved. For a while she could see Melinda's red shirt and then they were gone. She had dragged herself to a place where she could lean her back against a rock, and Damon had folded a jersey so that she could sit upon it, but at the best of times it is not too comfortable to sit on stone, and it was even worse now that she had to endure the pain in her ankle.

While the children had been with her, she had tried to be brave, especially not wanting to scare Adrian, who had regarded her with a small frightened face. But now that she was alone, she let go a little. Slow tears trickled down her cheeks and she wiped them away with the back of her hand. You're being stupid, she admonished herself. It isn't very late. It's still light and there's no danger. It's just a matter of waiting patiently. I wonder how long it will take before anyone can come for me? I hope they can send Mike, because I feel I'm being a nuisance, and at least I know him.

The pain in her ankle was increasing and she thought perhaps if she could crawl to a place near the stream and hold it in the ice-cold water this might help. It did help to a certain extent since after about ten minutes the ankle felt so numb it was practically anaesthetized. But then the pain began again and she began to feel stiff and bruised in other parts of her body. She crawled over to the rock again and tried to make herself more comfortable, then started to think how she could occupy the long time that she would have to wait before she could be rescued from her predicament.

There was a sudden sharp whistle that made her start. How wonderful it would be if she could see another walker, even if they could not help her to move. It would make her feel better just to have someone to talk to for a while. The sharp cry came again, but this time she noticed that it came from a ledge of rock some way above her. It was a hyrax or rock rabbit shouting to his companions from his place in the sun. The gorge was in shadow now, but the rocks were still lit with the sun of late afternoon and the little creatures were basking and taking advantage of the warmth before they bedded down in their holes.

Taryn occupied herself counting how many she could see and found that from dozens of vantage points they were staring down, keeping a keen watch upon her. It was quite unnerving, and yet what harm could they do to her? But now she was startled by a harsher noise, the threatening bark of a male baboon. There he sat high on a rock and she could see smaller ones, some mothers with babies on their backs, scrambling to get further away from her. She hoped they would continue to think of her as a threat, but, just in case of danger, she gathered some stones, though she would hate to have to use them.

She must have dozed for a while, because when she opened her eyes again, the sun had gone completely and the dark peaks showed jaggedly against the sky where a few stars were appearing. She had not felt particularly cold before, even though her clothes were damp, but now a chill wind blew up the gorge and she began to shake uncontrollably. She remembered too that Ross had said there were still leopards in this part of the country, and whenever she heard the rustle of vegetation, she thought of this danger. How she wished she could move around to get warm or that she had asked the children to collect some branches so that she could light a fire!

As it grew darker, she was several times deceived into thinking she saw a light in the distance, but then realized by the number of dancing sparks she saw around her that she was seeing fireflies further away amongst the trees. She felt now that with the pain and the cold she could easily lose control and have some kind of screaming hysterics, but she held firmly on to her desire not to show up too badly when Mike or some other ranger appeared, as she was sure they must.

But when at last she saw the golden glow of a light far off down the gorge, coming down the pathway through the trees, she started to weep through sheer relief. In the distance she heard the clip-clop of an animal, its hooves ringing against the rocks and then splashing as it negotiated the river. The lantern came nearer and she could distinguish horse and rider, dark figures in the gloom, just a little illuminated by the lantern and the light of the rising moon.

'Taryn, where the devil are you?'

It was the voice of Ross, echoing among the rocks.

'I'm here!' she shouted frantically.

Something like a searchlight shone upon her face and in a few minutes the mule had splashed across the shallow water and Ross was looking down at her.

'Well, here's a fine thing! I thought you told me you were quite grown-up and responsible. What the devil made you choose to come here and to try to cross that ladder, for heaven's sake?'

His angry impatience was the last straw and she sobbed bitterly, much to her own shame.

'Pull yourself together, Taryn. You told me you're not a child, so don't act like one. Let's have a look at this foot.'

67

Sobbing, she submitted her ankle to his inspection. His words had been harsh, but his touch was gentle. She looked at his dark head, glossy in the light of the torch, and wished desperately that it had been anyone else but he who had come to fetch her.

'It's very swollen,' she stammered, as he held the foot in his hand. 'I don't think I can get my sock and shoe on again.'

She was shivering, partly with cold and partly through nerves.

'Your foot is ice-cold. We shall have to try to put something on. I've brought a bandage and we'll fix it up as best we can for the journey home.' He produced the bandage and proceeded to put it on tightly and expertly. Taryn was still shivering violently.

'I've brought a towel and some dry clothes – Melinda had the sense to tell me you'd need them. Now take those wet things off and let's get you dried.'

'But I . . .'

'Oh, for crying out loud! This isn't the time to be modest. I'll walk away a few paces if that will satisfy you and I'll turn my back. But keep the torch, otherwise you won't be able to see to put them on.'

He strode away into the darkness and she struggled to divest herself of her wet clothes. It was terribly difficult because they clung damply to her body, and every twist and turn of her limbs increased the pain in her ankle. She tried to stand and the pain was so excruciating that she groaned aloud. She heard Ross's footsteps returning.

'Now look, Taryn, let me help you. Just pretend I'm a doctor or a robot or something. At this rate you're going to get pneumonia before we get back.'

He put the large towel around her, supporting her so she did not have to put any weight on her injured foot, and vigorously patted her dry.

'Now let me hold the towel around you and keep you steady while you put on some clothes,' he commanded. It was wonderful to feel the warmth of the thick fisherman-knit jersey he had brought.

'Whose is this?' she asked.

'Mine. One of those Aran knits from Scotland. The warmest garment I possess.'

She saw his smile in the torchlight.

'It's a trifle large for you, Taryn. Now sit down again and you shall have some hot coffee laced with brandy and a couple of pain-killing tablets before we tackle the ride back.'

He sat her against a rock and handed her a cup of scalding hot coffee from a flask. The sweetened beverage disguised the taste of the brandy which she knew she disliked, and she was so glad to be warm that she was prepared meekly to drink anything. A warm glow spread through her whole body and after a while the pain seemed to recede. Ross had sat down beside her and was holding the mug for her as if she were a child.

'I think I deserve some too,' he said.

A warm safe feeling flowed over her and she leaned her head against his shoulder, feeling as if she had found a refuge from all the pain and fear of the last hours. He laughed.

'Feeling sleepy?' he asked. 'That's all right. We shall soon have you home.'

'How am I going to get there?' she asked, yawning.

'You can sit on the mule and I'll lead you.'

He lifted her up and put her on the mule, sitting side-saddle.

'Are you all right like that?' he asked.

'Yes, I think so.'

He led the animal slowly along the path, shining the light to guard against taking it over rough places. The moon had come up, making silver shadows amongst the trees, and the pain in her ankle had stopped being quite so bad, for it was more firmly supported by the bandage. It had been reduced to a dull throbbing, not very pleasant, but made more remote by the effect of the tablets Ross had given her.

The path was smoother now, and this, together with the steady rhythm of the mule's pace, induced in her a hazy state so that it seemed she was riding in a dream. Her head

69

nodded and she kept having to jerk herself awake. When they came to a place where they had to cross the stream, Ross paused.

'You're going to fall off this animal if you can't keep awake. I'm coming up beside you to hold you on it.'

She was surprised into wakefulness.

'How can you do that? Together we shall be far too heavy.'

'You don't know these mountain mules. They're used to carrying great loads of provisions far heavier than our combined weights over the passes. Here it's level ground. I may weigh a ton, but you certainly don't.'

Taryn felt too weak to argue any more and in a moment he was up behind her, holding her to him as the mule, surprised by this sudden weight, pranced around before negotiating the shallow water. She leaned against him, hearing his heart beat beneath her head.

'There, that's better, isn't it?'

'Yes,' she said, 'much better.'

They rode on for a while in silence.

'I'm sorry,' she murmured.

'For what?' he asked.

'Sorry to have made a nuisance of myself. The only thing I'm thankful about is that it happened to me and not to one of the children.'

'Go to sleep. We'll talk about it tomorrow. Rest now. We only have a little distance to go before we reach the road and I've left the car there. We'll leave the mule to find his own way home.'

In the gorge during those lonely hours, Taryn had longed for home as if it had been a vision of heaven, but now she felt content to be with Ross, with the mule plodding along in its steady rhythm, his strong arms holding her close, and both of them in harmony with all differences smoothed away, at least until tomorrow.

CHAPTER FIVE

WHEN Taryn awoke next morning the sun was lighting up the gay colours of the patchwork quilt in her room. She lay for a few minutes hazily going over in her mind the events of yesterday. Her ankle still throbbed painfully and her sleep had been restless and haunted by dreams so that now she could not understand clearly what was true or false in her recollections. Small scenes flashed through her brain. She remembered how she had found herself in the doorway supported by Ross, how the children had rushed forward to greet her and how, collapsing on the chair that Damon had brought, she had looked up and seen Coral standing in the living-room, an expression of annoyance flashing from those emerald eyes. Or had she imagined this? For afterwards Coral had been sweetly sympathetic in her own way.

'What bad luck,' she had said silkily. 'But of course you were not to know how dangerous the gorge can be. Indeed she was fortunate, wasn't she, Ross, that an afternoon storm didn't break and bring the river down? That could easily have happened. I should have thought you would have read the guide to the district in which it warns you about that. When you're looking after children, you can't be too careful, I always think.'

Adrian had glared at her, his blue eyes angry.

'Taryn looked after us well. She would have been fine if that stupid ladder hadn't given way.'

'Well, of course, Adrian. Dear me, Taryn, you've made one conquest at any rate!'

Ross did not seem to be listening.

'Melinda,' he said, 'you can come and help Taryn to get to bed. But go first to ask Mrs. Fuller for a hot water bottle. I'll carry you up the stairs, Taryn.'

'But you can't do that!'

'I can and I will. You're pretty lightweight.'

Now she thought, lightweight? I suppose I am. Not only

71

physically but all round. Everything I've done so far seems to have ended badly. If only I could do something right for once!

She remembered being carried up the stairs in his arms and being deposited gently into a chair.

'There, Taryn, that will do until Melinda comes with your hot water bottle and helps you into bed. I shall come later to rebandage the ankle.'

Melinda had only just finished helping her when Ross reappeared.

'Go and see if you can rustle up some soup and toast and chicken or scrambled egg for Taryn from Mrs. Fuller. Meanwhile I'll see to the ankle.'

He unwrapped the makeshift bandage and did a much more professional job.

'How do you know how to do this kind of thing?' she asked, amazed at the way his deft long brown fingers dealt with the yards of bandage.

'You have to know about first aid when you wander around in wild places as I do,' he replied. 'There, does that feel better?'

'Much,' she answered, smiling at him. He replaced the coverlet and took her hand in his.

'You've been a sweet, brave girl and I'm sorry I snapped at you. I guess I was worried. After all, you are very young and in my care.'

He's still regarding me as a child, thought Taryn. But before she could respond to him, he heard Melinda and got up to open the door for her.

'Thanks, Melinda, you've been a great help.' He put his arm around her and gave her an affectionate pat, and she smiled radiantly. 'Now just go and see that Adrian gets to bed, will you? He insisted on staying up past his bedtime because he was so anxious about you, Taryn.'

He turned towards the bed with the tray he had taken from Melinda. 'Now what's here?'

'I really don't feel hungry,' Taryn protested.

'You must have something.'

Ross stood over her and insisted on her drinking the cup

of soup and eating a little of the creamed chicken and toast. She felt even more like a child as he bullied her into taking just a little more than she really wanted. Then he gave her a sleeping tablet with a cup of hot milk.

'Sleep well,' he said. 'Tomorrow you're going to feel fine.'

As he patted the sheet, Taryn plucked up courage and took his hand.

'Thank you for everything,' she said.

Coral's voice came from the doorway.

'For heaven's sake, Ross! I'm sure Taryn needs to rest. And dinner has been waiting for ages. Mrs. Fuller is furious.'

Now, this morning, Taryn was determined to get up and not give Mrs. Fuller any further reason to grumble. Her ankle, firmly bandaged, felt easier and her walking stick was in the room, so she managed to hobble to the bathroom, which was en suite with her room, and wash and dress, putting on slacks and a pullover as being the easiest garments to wear. She could only wear one shoe, but that hardly mattered as she could not put her foot properly to the ground.

She hobbled along to the children's rooms, but found them uninhabited by their owners and looking unnaturally neat. So she started a kind of dot-and-carry-one progression down the stairs. She could hear laughter and children's voices together with the deeper tone of Ross's voice coming from the dining-room, and she managed to make her slow way to the bottom without anyone hearing her. But when she appeared at the door there was a sudden silence and she was conscious of four pairs of surprised eyes gazing at her. Ross jumped to his feet and helped her to a chair.

'Taryn, for crying out loud, I thought you were still asleep in bed. You shouldn't have battled downstairs. Mrs. Fuller could have brought your breakfast up.'

'Thank you, I can manage quite well now, I hope, and you've all been marvellous,' she said, turning to Melinda, Damon and Adrian. 'Your rooms look so neat.'

They looked at each other and laughed.

'Ross made us do it,' said Adrian. 'Please, Taryn, get

73

better soon.'

'So that you have a handmaid?' asked Ross. 'Really, Taryn, you must make them more independent.'

That's what I was trying to do yesterday, thought Taryn, and look what happened then! But she did not say it aloud. Mrs. Fuller came into the room.

'Good morning, Miss Bartlett, I'm glad to see you're feeling better.' She looked anything but glad. 'Miss Swann has rung for her tray, so I came to see if Melinda could take it. I'm run off my feet with all this extra work.'

Melinda got to her feet quite willingly and promptly. Taryn thought that she was proving much more helpful than had seemed likely when she first met her.

'I'll come in a minute,' she told Mrs. Fuller. 'I just want to go outside for something . . . er . . . a geranium from the windowbox to put on Coral's tray.'

'Just take it up, child,' said Ross rather sharply. 'There's no time for frills this morning.'

But Melinda had gone. Adrian began to giggle for no apparent reason.

'What's the matter, Adrian?'

Ross, by no means a patient man, seemed to have had enough of the children's company at breakfast.

'I just thought of something funny,' said Adrian. 'But I can't tell anyone.'

'Well, if you can't share the joke, stop being so tiresome, and get down from the table if you've finished. Taryn, would you like to sit in the sun on the verandah for a while?'

'Yes, that would be very pleasant,' Taryn replied. 'If Damon and Adrian bring one of their games, I can keep them amused.'

But they had hardly settled down when Mike Murray drove up in the truck.

'What's Mike doing here so early?' asked Ross, and strode out to see him. They chatted together for a while, and Taryn thought what a contrast they made, Ross with his dark hair and aquiline profile and his lean lithe frame that had a grace all its own, and Mike, red-haired, strong-looking and sturdy,

74

but a carthorse compared with the other man's racehorse good looks. They both came in and Mike took Taryn's hand, holding it close as if to convey his sympathy.

'I had no idea you'd met with an accident, Miss Bartlett. I came to see if I could take you and the children for a drive as far as a Bushman cave. I have to check up on a herd of eland that are on the hillside there and I thought it might be a novelty for you to see the paintings.'

'That's so kind of you,' said Taryn, attempting to release her hand but finding it firmly enclosed in his. 'I'm afraid I couldn't do that today, as you can see.'

'But there's no reason why you shouldn't take the children,' said Ross heartily. He stared at Mike, who suddenly became conscious that he was holding Taryn's hand and dropped it hastily. 'I'm sure they would like to go to the cave and they would be interested in seeing the eland. I think we can guarantee their good behaviour, can't we, Taryn?'

'Of course they can come,' said Mike, 'but I'm sorry Miss Bartlett . . .'

'Please call me Taryn. It's easier. After all, you said I could call you Mike.'

'Well, that's settled, then,' said Ross, somewhat brusquely. 'Will they need a packed lunch?'

'No. I've got enough food in the truck.'

It seemed only a few seconds before the children were installed in the truck and it was disappearing into the distance. Even Melinda had seemed eager to go, although she had said previously that she would be glad of a day at home. Taryn found herself alone with Ross on the verandah. He grinned engagingly.

'Was that bad of me, Taryn?'

His blue eyes were dark with sparkling laughter.

'What do you mean?'

'I mean that obviously Mike has taken a fancy to you and was using the children as an excuse to take you out for the day, and now the poor man is landed with the three of them and no girl-friend.'

'I don't think for a moment that it was how you say,'

Taryn said in some embarrassment. 'Mike seems a kind sort of man and he was thinking of the children's amusement. And how can you refer to me as his girl-friend?' she added indignantly. 'I've only met the man once before.'

'I know the signs,' said Ross.

'From long experience, I suppose,' Taryn snapped.

'Now don't be cross with me. Think how much more restful it will be with the children out for the day. You can tell how beautifully quiet it can be.'

It was true, thought Taryn. It was a sunny day and the air was blue in the heavens except where the white mist of morning was disappearing from the peaks. The only sounds were the calls of the cormorants by the river and the rustling of the wind in the grass. Suddenly this peaceful silence was broken by a high scream. They looked at each other, startled.

'Good God, that's Coral,' exclaimed Ross, and was off into the house and up the stairs. Taryn waited nervously. She heard Mrs. Fuller calling and then going up at a slower pace. What could be the matter? Oh, if only this wretched ankle were better! Taryn felt frightened, frustrated and thoroughly alarmed.

Then, much to her surprise, she heard Ross laughing, and Coral's voice raised in anger. She went on speaking for some time and Taryn could hear Ross's voice too, but could not make out the words. Then she heard Mrs. Fuller descending the stairs. She came on to the verandah obviously aching to tell someone what had happened.

'That Melinda!' she exclaimed. 'She's a little madam and no mistake. Miss Swann swears she put it there and she must be right. It couldn't have got there on its own.'

'What is it?' asked Taryn.

'A lizard, one of those big ones with a blue head. It was in the drawer when Miss Swann went to get her clothes. She says Melinda had a packet with her and she heard it rustle when she asked her to get her bedjacket out. Well, Miss Swann's in a proper state. I knew they'd both got hot tempers when they were roused, but I've never seen her like this before. She says Mr. Trent has got to send those children to school straight away. I can't say I should care. I've always thought it was a crazy idea to bring them here. If they go it will suit me.'

She went back to the kitchen and Taryn was left to her thoughts. The blueheaded lizard, that fascinating, revolting animal they had seen in the gorge! It must be the same. Melinda must have carried it in a packet and brought it home to play a trick on Coral. Of course she had said she wished she would go, and Taryn remembered how determined she had sounded. But according to Mrs. Fuller this might have the opposite effect. I wonder what's happening upstairs, she thought. She would soon know. Meanwhile Coral's voice was growing louder. It sounded as if she had come out of her room and was striding up and down the passage.

'Put some clothes on, Coral,' she heard Ross say. 'You'll catch cold in that flimsy nightgown.'

'A lot you care if I do! I tell you, Ross, I've reached the limit of my patience with this crazy set-up. It's senseless for a bachelor like you to take on three children. They should be at school, and the sooner the better.'

'But I've told you, Coral. You can't just fling them into strange schools until they've settled down and become used to the country. The syllabus will be strange and new. I've engaged a young teacher to come and coach them. This set-up won't last for long, I promise you.'

'Well, I hope for your sake the young teacher is a bit more competent than Taryn. I know you thought you had to have someone to bring them here, though personally I think that was quite unnecessary, but now she is here, she seems to give you more trouble than the children.'

'I'm not prepared to argue about it, Coral. I think you must admit that Mrs. Fuller wouldn't be willing to do the extra work, and there'll be occasions when I have to leave them and do business trips.'

Coral's voice was high and shrewish.

'I'm glad to hear you do mean to leave them sometimes! The way things look at the moment one would think you were glued here by Taryn's fatal charm. If I didn't know

77

that you can't stand plain women, I should be inclined to be jealous, but as it is, I have no qualms about leaving here today. I'm thoroughly sick of the whole scene! I'm going to catch that luxury bus you were so eager to tell me about, and if you'll take me into the village, I'll catch it today. When you're prepared to lead a more civilized life you can phone me and let me know. But don't expect me to hang around waiting for you. You aren't the only one on my mailing list, Ross, and you should know that by now!'

Ross's voice was cold as steel. Taryn shivered as she heard it. 'Thank you for letting me know. As far as I'm concerned, Coral, you're quite at liberty to do what you like, and so, may I add, am I. As soon as you've packed and dressed, I'll drive you to the bus. I'm afraid I can't offer to take you to Durban in the present circumstances.'

Coral gave a high sneering laugh.

'I suppose you'd intended to spend the day holding the nursemaid's hand. Too bad I've interrupted your plan.'

'Don't be ridiculous, Coral. You might as well accuse me of having an interest in Melinda.'

Taryn could hear him stamping down the stairs. And then he came out on to the verandah. He was scowling, his eyes black with rage. She did not know what to say, feeling that whatever she said it would be the wrong thing.

'I'm taking Coral to the bus. She's decided to leave,' he said, apparently unaware that the quarrel had resounded all over the house. 'By the way, where did Melinda get the creature?'

'We saw it in the gorge, but I didn't know she had it. It must have been when she and Adrian were alone that they caught it.'

'That accounts for Adrian's giggles at breakfast. I shouldn't have thought Melinda capable of doing anything so childish. It's true the sooner they can be sent to school, the better. They'll probably get out of hand left to themselves here.'

He isn't impressed with my ability to supervise them, that's one one thing certain, thought Taryn drearily. As soon as they were sent to school, obviously she would have to leave

78

and find another job or go back to England.

'Well, while we're going to the village, we may as well take you to let the doctor have a look at that ankle,' Ross went on. 'Do you feel up to it?'

'Yes, but . . .' Taryn wanted to say, 'What will Coral have to say?' but in the face of Ross's frowning expression, she could only murmur meekly, 'If you think I should, certainly I can manage it.'

'It won't take long. I'll leave you at the doctor's surgery, while I take Coral to her bus, then call back for you. I'll just tell Mrs. Fuller we shall all be out for lunch.'

Coral was furious when she found Taryn was coming too. Hardly a word was spoken as they drove through the pleasant valley in the direction of the little town and away from the hills. Taryn knew that this icy silence was on account of her presence and she wondered whether perhaps it was a good thing that she had come. Otherwise they might have quarrelled again, and it would not have been good for Ross's driving to get into another rage. On the other hand, there might have been a reconciliation. Who knows?

When Coral started to talk, it seemed to be as much for Taryn's benefit as for Ross's, for she spoke of the modelling jobs she had been offered and the marvellous round of parties she was expecting to attend.

'Your friends will be missing you, Ross. Already when I came away everyone was asking what had become of you.' She turned to Taryn. 'You wouldn't know, Taryn, of course, but Ross is simply fantastic at parties. He dances fabulously and he's a very good host.'

'Thanks for those few kind words,' said Ross.

'Do you remember when I acted hostess for you at that huge party you gave for those V.I.P.s from America? It was a wonderful affair, wasn't it? Do you remember my silver dress? You said I looked gorgeous.'

'And so you did,' Ross answered.

She's trying to make up a bit now, thought Taryn. And maybe she's trying to put me in my place by showing me how important Ross is. But what could I care? It really has nothing to do with me. She just used me during the quarrel to fan his rage. And, as he said, it was rather ridiculous.

She remembered his words, 'You might as well accuse me of having an interest in Melinda.' Well, after hearing that, Taryn did not need Coral to put her in her place. She knew she was well and truly there holding a very low position in Ross's opinion, as childish as Melinda without her young charm, childish in her actions when she should be more responsible. And the deep emotion she remembered experiencing during that ride home, held closely and thrillingly in his arms, were all part of a misty dream like the white wraiths upon the blue mountain tops that vanished so swiftly at the coming up of the sun. And like the morning mists it was best forgotten, because how much better it was to be able to see clearly.

What else was there for her, Taryn, but to be practical? She had left those posts in London because she had felt that there must be more to life than doing monotonous things in boring surroundings. She had longed for a more exciting existence in glamorous circumstances. Well, now she was getting it and she should be delighted. Then why did she feel so sad? Was it perhaps because she longed to prove herself competent? If this was so, she must do her best to succeed. A life such as Coral and Ross led was not for her. She could only stand on the outside looking in. And she must forget the hurt she had felt when Coral said that about Ross not liking plain women, forget the twinge of envy when she looked at Coral's perfect features. What did that matter so long as she could settle here and manage to hold down the job for as long as it lasted?

By the time they arrived in the small town, Coral and Ross seemed to be speaking fairly amiably to each other. Ross deposited Taryn at the doctor's surgery with instructions to wait there until he returned. She could hardly do anything else, could she? The doctor confirmed that the ankle was merely sprained and commended Ross's bandaging. There was little she could do except rest and it would gradually recover.

She sat outside on a seat enjoying the sun and watching the activity in the main street. It was like a frontier town in a Wild West film, she thought, except that there were Africans with colourful blankets on their shoulders, riding their small sturdy horses in the dusty streets, or forming in talkative groups in front of the main trading stores. The shops were attractive in an odd old-fashioned way; decorative pediments had been added to the roofs and the exteriors painted in bright pink, yellow and green. She was so interested that she did not notice the passing of time and was quite surprised when she saw Ross's car draw up in front of the surgery.

'Coral caught a bus and was well satisfied with her seat,' he told her.

'I'm sorry Melinda angered her with that trick,' said Taryn. She seemed to be spending her life saying sorry for one thing or another.

'Coral is soon angered and just as soon reconciled,' said Ross. 'Think nothing of it. She would have had to go soon anyhow, with all these modelling dates and parties on hand.'

He's so arrogant, Taryn thought. I was stupid to be touched by his apparent kindness over my accident. It was just the casual care he would have shown to any child who had been hurt. But I can't stand the way he speaks as if he holds Coral in the palm of his hand, as if he just has to wait and any woman would run to do his bidding. He seems without feeling and not affected at all by his angry quarrel. Can he love her? Or does he love only himself and thinks of Coral as a useful beautiful hostess and future wife, who will be a proud possession to own?

Some miles from the centre of the town, they drew up at a small wayside restaurant where there were tables outside in the garden but shaded by gay umbrellas. The people who were already there looked curiously at her as Ross helped her to a seat, and she could not help remembering how he had said that any man liked to take a beautiful woman with him. Well, now all heads were turning towards her, but for a much more mundane reason.

The waitress came forward to help move the chair for Taryn and said, 'Shame, has your wife hurt her leg, sir?'

Ross laughed at Taryn's expression.

'Someone at any rate thinks you look old enough to be married, Taryn.' Then turning to the waitress, 'What have you got for us? How about that good grilled steak I had here last time with a green salad? And yes, this time I think we can order French fried potatoes. I'm sure you aren't watching your weight, are you, Taryn?'

She shook her head. It was clear that the last time he had eaten here, he had been with Coral, for she considered everything she ate in the light of whether it would put on a few ounces. But she tried not to think of this but simply to enjoy the unaccustomed treat of having a well served meal in novel surroundings. She looked around, appreciating the attractive garden, the green lawns, the feathery bamboo palms, creaking even in this slight breeze, the odd-shaped papaya trees with their long stems and golden fruit placed just under the green fingers of the foliage, the hibiscus bushes splashed red with their flowers, and the magenta clusters of the bougainvillea spilling over its trellis.

'It's so pretty here,' she said, turning to Ross, and found that he was regarding her with an intent expression in his dark blue eyes.

'I find my own view remarkably pretty too,' he said. Taryn looked back at him in astonishment.

'Why should you look so amazed?' he asked. 'Am I not allowed to pay a compliment to a pretty girl?'

'Only if you're sincere,' Taryn replied.

She could still remember the hurt of Coral's words during their quarrel. Did Ross realize she had heard Coral call her plain and was that why he was pretending admiration?

'Of course I'm sincere,' Ross declared. 'It's so delightful to watch your expression when you don't know anyone is observing you. You were looking so charmed with your surroundings. It's good to be with a girl who's pleased by little things for a change.'

Of course that was it. He was annoyed by Coral's desertion and so had decided to amuse himself by emphasizing the contrast between herself and Coral. He was pretending to admire her lack of sophistication, but really what he was used to was beauty and elegance in women.

She was saved from further reflection by the arrival of the steak, grilled to tender perfection. She ate hungrily finding that her appetite had returned, and she enjoyed the glass of rose-coloured wine that was served with the meal.

'This is so good. It's the first time I've ever had a meal in a garden restaurant,' she informed him.

He looked at her in astonishment.

'But, my child, what have you been doing with yourself all your life? Surely even in London or . . . haven't you ever been to the Continent?'

'I've done nothing,' said Taryn, ashamed that she must confess to such an uninteresting life. 'I've been to school, started training as a nurse, was called back to nurse my grandparents, held boring jobs until I got rid of them or they got rid of me and – well, that's the story of my life.'

He questioned her more about her life previous to coming here and she found herself talking quite freely to him.

'And you wanted a little excitement and grabbed at the chance of this job because you thought you'd find it here in South Africa? Poor girl, have you been disappointed?'

Why did his smile hold such charm, she thought, when he, with the arrogance of his wealth and power, could mock her so easily?

'Not disappointed, no,' she said. 'I'm fascinated by what I've seen of the country up to now. Strange as it may seem to you, although I've never before known mountain country, it appeals to me enormously.'

'Good, I'm glad of that,' he said abruptly. 'So far, so good. You know, of course, that once the children have gone to school, there'll be no need for your services any more, but doubtless we can find something for you to do, though I can't promise it will be amongst the mountains. Now, where's that waitress? We must get on.'

She felt rebuffed. Why had he been questioning her if he found her conversation so boring? She had been feeling so happy and now she felt let down. But when he came from the inside of the building where he had been paying for the meal, he was smiling.

'Look here, I've got something I thought might appeal to you.'

He had noticed on the counter a collection of small animals carved by Africans and had bought a tiny tortoise for her.

'One slowcoach for another,' he said, helping her to hobble to the car. 'That's what I like to see, a smile that reaches to your eyes. You were looking so sad and serious while you were waiting for me at the table.'

All the way home Taryn held the smooth little tortoise closely in her hands and every now and again stole a glimpse at it in secret delight.

'You're like a child with a new toy,' said Ross, catching her at this.

But I must prove to him that I'm not a child, she thought.

CHAPTER SIX

A WEEK later, Ross announced one morning that he expected the tutor to arrive next day. Meanwhile Taryn's ankle had healed quite quickly and she was able to go for short walks. Ross had engaged a string of mountain ponies and he took the children upon several trails along the hillsides.

'Is he arriving by bus? Can we go to meet him?' Melinda asked.

'Are you so eager to go into the village?' asked Ross. 'Bad luck, Melinda, he's coming in his own car. I've given directions how to get here. Taryn, could you warn Mrs. Fuller that there'll be an extra person for meals in future, and perhaps you could see that his room is prepared? Not the gold room, but the other one in my wing.'

The gold room seemed to be reserved for Coral, who was making her absence felt by constantly phoning Ross usually at awkward times, when they were sitting down to a meal or else late at night. Taryn had thought at first it must be costly for her to make all these calls and that she must love Ross very dearly, but she realized later from something that was said that she reversed the charges.

'Another person, and a young man at that,' Mrs. Fuller grumbled when Taryn went into the kitchen. 'I expect he'll have a large appetite and want snacks at all hours. It's really too much for me. I didn't undertake to do all this when Mr. Trent engaged me.'

'I wish you'd let me help you,' said Taryn.

Mrs. Fuller was very obstinate about allowing Taryn into the kitchen. She seemed to prefer to grumble and do things her own way, although Ross had engaged a cousin of Moses' to help with the rough work. But she was not above suggesting that Taryn was unwilling to help her, especially when she was speaking to Ross. Taryn often felt rather despairing about the whole situation. She tried to keep the children occupied and out of the way as much as possible and she used the laundry to do their washing and prepared the lunches for them when they went out for the day. But when the teacher arrived and the children were more occupied, Taryn thought she would not have enough to do, for the African servants were quite capable of doing the small domestic tasks that she did now.

Melinda, Damon and Adrian remained in the house during the afternoon next day instead of wandering off for a walk or down to the place where the horses were stabled. At about four o'clock their patience was rewarded by the sight of a red sports car, whizzing up the hill taking the hairpin bends at a great speed. Near the front door it came to a sudden halt, and a young man, his long brown hair rather tousled, stepped over the car door and swung a suitcase after him.

'He looks all right,' said Damon, standing at his point of observation right up against the window.

'Mmm . . .' Melinda agreed from a more discreet place. 'I think he may do. For heaven's sake, get away from the window, Damon. He'll see you.'

'So what?' asked Damon. 'He's going to see a lot more of me during the next few weeks.'

'I mean he'll think we're a lot of quizzy kids.'

'Well, aren't we?' Adrian piped up.

'I wonder where he got those blue jeans,' asked Melinda. 'I'd give anything for some in that fabulous faded colour.'

'You can ask him,' said Damon.

'Isn't anyone going to let him in?' asked Taryn, but the children were all suddenly overcome with shyness and it was left to her to open the door.

Allister Harding was a good-looking young man with mid-brown hair worn long and a rather romantic-looking moustache worn with sideburns. His grey eyes were wide and intelligent, and he smiled as Taryn opened the door.

'Hello, are you one of my pupils? If so, I'm in luck.'

Well, he doesn't waste much time, thought Taryn. But I suppose he's trying to create a good impression.

'No, no, I'm afraid I'm a little old for school,' she said. 'Here they are, all waiting to meet you.'

Taryn felt quite envious of the way Allister settled in so well. It was easier for him, she supposed. He knew what his duties were and kept the children well occupied during the morning with their different lessons. He himself was studying for extra qualifications, he told Taryn, and had been glad to get this job which afforded some free time and was paid well. He had such easy charm that even Mrs. Fuller forgot to grumble. Taryn herself felt that she was becoming quite redundant.

As soon as Ross had seen that the children had settled down well with Allister, he had gone off to Durban on business and said he would not be back for a few days. She had not realized how much she had come to rely on his presence, how much she had unconsciously looked forward to seeing that infectious smile that reached up to the dark blue eyes when he was laughing with the children. She tried not to think in this way. How could she miss him like this when his presence made her feel awkward and in the wrong?

She had another worry too while Ross was absent. From the first Melinda seemed to have been attracted to Allister and it was no wonder, for he was gay and charming and young. Allister had been discreet and not shown any interest while Ross was there to observe him, but in his absence he relaxed his guard and seemed to give Melinda every encouragement in her girlish attempts to attract him. Taryn wondered whether she should speak to Allister. He would probably tell her it was no business of hers, but she felt responsible for Melinda in the absence of Ross.

She had noticed that Allister and Melinda had become accustomed to sit in front of the fireplace on a deep settee after the boys had gone to bed. Often Taryn had tasks to do, milky drinks to prepare for Adrian or a story to read to him, so she was forced to leave them alone and felt a little uneasy about it. But tonight she was determined to outsit Melinda, so she returned to the living-room when she had persuaded Adrian to accept a shorter story.

They were sitting rather close together and Allister seemed to drop Melinda's hand when she came in.

'Have you finished already, Taryn?' asked Melinda, not sounding too pleased.

'Yes, and I intend to sit up until midnight if necessary, because I want to finish my knitting,' said Taryn, producing a jersey she had started for Adrian.

'Surely there's no hurry,' Melinda protested, frowning. 'It's so hot most of the time here.'

'But it's cold in the evenings, and in any case, as you know, my time here may be limited.'

After a while Melinda, yawning, tacitly admitted defeat and said she intended to go to bed. Allister stayed on. Soon he came over to sit on the arm of Taryn's chair, leaning over pretending to inspect the pattern, but putting his face close to her hair.

'Do you have to do that, Taryn? It drives me crazy seeing you clicking away like those women at the guillotine in the French Revolution. Put it away for a few minutes and be sociable.' He got up to switch on the record player.

'Don't do that. You'll disturb the children.'

'Is that all you think of? I like to have background music. It gives a romantic atmosphere.'

'I can't think what you want that for,' said Taryn crisply. 'Turn it down a bit.'

'Oh, very well. Anyone would think you were the school-teacher, not me.'

He came back to sit on the arm of her chair.

'Why did you say your time here was limited?'

'There's very little necessity for my presence now you're here. You must see that.'

'But why bother to leave? My duties certainly don't include making milky drinks and telling stories or knitting jerseys. I should think you're worth your salary, and our boss is stinking rich. He can afford to pay you. I'm sorry I didn't ask for more money. In fact I think I shall when he comes back from his money-grubbing in the city.'

'Do you like Ross?' asked Taryn, curious to know what the young man's opinion was.

'Like? You don't use such tame words about a person like him. He's damnably arrogant and wealthy. Men envy him, including me, and women are charmed – or hadn't you noticed? Imagine having all that money and personal magnetism as well. I should think it would be a fate worse than death to fall in love with him. So you'd better steer clear, Taryn, or have you succumbed already? Sure that's not why you want to leave?'

'Of course not,' Taryn denied hotly.

'There's no future for you with him. Look in my direction. I'm a much better bet if you like a mild flutter with no wedding bells in mind.'

He was leaning over her chair, laughing into her eyes. She got up and moved away from him.

'Allister, I don't take you seriously, but a younger girl might. Be careful with Melinda.'

He laughed merrily. He himself had a great deal of charm, she thought.

'How can you say such a thing? I know Melinda is just a little girl. But you must admit it appeals to a man's vanity to see those huge beautiful blue eyes gazing at him as if he were the greatest thing since Paul Newman.'

'Please don't give her any ideas, Allister. Young girls can get hurt easily.'

'What about older ones?'

She was standing and their eyes were on a level. His were twinkling with mischief.

'Come on, Taryn, let's stop being serious. I promise I'll forget Melinda if you'll take pity on me.'

He turned up the player and seizing her in his arms waltzed her around the room.

'There, wasn't that pleasant?'

He put his arms around her and before she could stop him he was kissing her. There was a cough or some other noise from the doorway and there stood Ross. The music had disguised the noise of the car's arrival.

'You both look well occupied,' he observed.

'Ross . . . we weren't expecting you until tomorrow.'

'That's pretty obvious. I finished the business early and so decided to get back here. Pour me a whisky, Allister, there's a good chap. And Taryn, I wonder if you could rustle up an omelette. I haven't eaten since lunchtime.'

She was glad to have an excuse to get away. In the kitchen she broke eggs, heated the frying pan, made toast, started the percolator, quite automatically, all the time feeling uncomfortable that Ross had witnessed the scene. But there was nothing she could have done to prevent it. Allister obviously liked to try his chances with any female who happened to be available. She put the coffee on the hot tray to simmer and wheeled in the trolley with the hot omelette, a small green salad and the toast. Allister had discreetly disappeared.

'That looks good, Taryn. Have a nightcap with me.'

'I'll have some coffee later,' Taryn replied, refusing his offer. Ross did not say another word until he had finished and she had poured the hot coffee, then stretching his legs out to the fire, which he had renewed with a fresh log, he said, 'Who taught you to make such a superb omelette? It's much better than Mrs. Fuller's.'

'I know how to cook simple things,' she replied.

'Did you know that on Mont St. Michel there's a monument to the memory of Mère Poulard who was famed for her omelettes? Doesn't seem too appropriate, somehow, to commemorate in granite such a light, soft thing as an omelette, does it?'

When is he going to come to the point? thought Taryn. He must have been displeased to come in on that scene. I wonder what he thought?

'How have things been going while I've been away? Do the children seem interested in this school work?' he asked.

'Yes. They all seem to have taken to Allister very well. He seems a good teacher.'

'And you ... you seem to have taken to him rather well yourself. I suppose I should have foreseen that.'

It was better, thought Taryn, that Ross should think that she was the one who interested Allister. He would be furious if he were to discover that Allister had been flirting with Melinda. But he must not find out. She hoped that she had warned Allister off sufficiently. She must let Ross go on thinking that she and Allister were attracted to each other.

'He's a very charming, intelligent young man,' she said. 'I find his company enjoyable. I've had little chance in my life to meet men of my own age.'

'In that case I think you should be more careful. You're very young for your years, Taryn. Don't be carried away by a quick attraction.'

'I'll try not to. But, Ross, I think how I feel is my own business.'

There was a sudden flash of anger in his dark blue eyes.

'Don't be so sure. While you're under my roof, Taryn, it concerns your employer as well. Besides, I don't want the children to be disturbed by being witnesses to a love affair, or their teacher to be distracted by one.'

His anger struck an answering heat in her response to him.

'How dare you say such a thing? It's you who are emphasizing it too much. Just because you saw Allister kissing me it doesn't mean to say we regarded it seriously. It was nothing of the kind. Can't two people find each other attractive without plunging immediately into a romantic love affair?'

He looked angrier still. 'I owe you an apology, it seems. I didn't realize that you were the type who would take a man's kisses so lightly. It seems you're well able to take care of yourself. But all the same, you may not have so much experience as to know that something started as a light flirtation often gets out of hand.'

'It won't in this case, I assure you. Allister is a charming young man, but I would never take him seriously.'

'Who then would you take seriously? An honest Joe like Mike, perhaps. He seems as if he would make good husband material, if you could stand the boredom of being a ranger's wife.'

'I know very little about Mike, and Ross, believe me, I am not, as you seem to think, in search of a husband. I value my freedom, and I'm still young.'

And that should settle this cross-examination, thought

Taryn. Now he had come back, she felt nothing but enmity for this man who sat regarding her across the coffee table with probing dark blue glances. How could she have thought she missed him when he was away? We're much happier without him, she thought.

'May I clear away now?' she asked.

'Why, certainly,' he said, sounding very cool and annoyed.

He got up to help her with the food trolley, but she refused, saying she could manage quite well on her own. Suddenly he smiled.

'What's wrong, Taryn? Why are you looking so grim?'

Really, he was impossible!

'Grim? It's you who've been grim ever since you came home. Even though I work for you, it doesn't give you any right to dictate to me about my personal life, but you'll be pleased to hear that I'm not interested in any man I've met since I came here, so I don't intend to distract Allister by flirting with him.'

'I must say I would have thought otherwise when I came in. You looked very interested in Allister then. But when you declare so fervently that you're not interested in any man you've met since you came here, does that imply that you have someone in England?'

'Maybe,' said Taryn, thinking that this story might end the discussion. 'But I don't choose to tell you anything about it.'

That can keep him guessing, she thought, as she put the plates in the dishwasher. What an aggravating man he is! I should be very glad to leave and never see him again if only I could think of some way to do it. She thought of those emotions she seemed to have imagined the time when she sprained her ankle. How silly and sentimental she had been! It had all been caused no doubt by the frightening experience she had just endured.

While they were having breakfast next morning, the phone rang and Ross went to answer it.

'It was for you,' he told Taryn. 'Mike was on the line and he asked me if you were free to go with him on some expedition. I told him the children were doing lessons but that I thought you could come.'

Taryn was not too pleased at this high-handed treatment. She thought she could have been consulted in case she wanted to refuse. Now it was not possible. She would have to go if Ross had said she could, but Mrs. Fuller would have plenty to say about her neglect of her duties. She always seemed to find herself placed in a difficult position.

She found, however, that she thoroughly enjoyed the time with Mike. They went in the truck for quite a way up a mountain and then walked so that they should not disturb the game that Mike was trying to count.

'We've reintroduced the types of antelope that used to be here in the old days when settlers first came. They were shot out by the hunters and it's only in recent years that we've been able to get them to breed in any great numbers,' he explained. 'Now we have another problem. The eland, which are very large, are breeding too fast for the quantity of grass that's needed to feed them. It's all right in the summer when we've had rain, but in the winter there's little grazing. I'm making a count of them so that we can decide if we need to get rid of some to other reserves in Africa.'

'How do you manage to count them?' asked Taryn.

'It's a matter of luck and observation. This morning, for instance, I'm after a large herd that one of the Africans reported is in this vicinity. I want us to try to come up quietly on them and then you can help me count.'

It was still early enough to see the small tracks of buck and rabbits over the damp grass, and overhead in a pale blue sky the eagles circled in effortless flight. Across the hillsides, Taryn saw the small wild flowers of Africa, pink and blue harebells, red ixia, the yellow fire lily. Mike, who had been scanning the landscape with his glasses, grasped her arm.

'There on the skyline,' he said.

She could see the outline of several large animals.

'Let's try to get closer,' Mike suggested. 'We must do it quietly. We'll have to crouch down.'

They crawled over rocks, shinned panting up the hillsides, trying to remain hidden in the long grass. Finally they

93

managed to come within fifty yards of the herd without disturbing them.

'Oh, they're magnificent!' breathed Taryn.

There they stood, score upon score of eland, the largest antelope in Africa.

'Some of the bulls can weigh up to fifteen hundred pounds,' said Mike.

'Are they dangerous?' asked Taryn. They looked so huge, and Mike did not even carry a gun.

'No, they're gentle beasts.'

When she inspected them through the glasses, Taryn found that indeed they did look gentle, with large brown eyes and pale gold pelts, cowlike, but much more handsome than cows. They counted seventy-five in the herd.

'Too many,' said Mike. 'I'd like to get farmers interested in taking some of them over. Their meat could satisfy hordes of hungry Africans if we could only get people accustomed to the idea.'

'You're horribly practical,' said Taryn. 'I much prefer to look at them and admire them. I hate to think of them as meat.'

They were sitting in the shelter of a rock and the herd was moving slowly beyond the ridge.

'You're a sweet thing,' said Mike. 'Are you glad you came with me today, Taryn?'

'Very glad,' Taryn answered. 'I was feeling rather depressed this morning before you phoned.'

'Why was that?'

'I suppose it's just that since Allister came, I have less to do for the children and I feel rather superfluous. I should start looking around for some other post.'

'Do you like this part of the country?'

'More than I can say. Not that I've seen much else of South Africa, of course.'

'Then why not stay?'

'How can I? It's awful to feel you aren't earning what's paid to you. And Mrs. Fuller makes me feel a bit useless.'

'She looks a bit of an old gorgon to me. I shouldn't take any notice of her. But I didn't mean you should stay there. A clerical job is coming up with the Parks Board soon. It's not very difficult, just looking after the office a bit, seeing to bookings and helping around the place. I'm sure you could do it. Usually the other ranger's wife would do it, but she hasn't been very well.'

'I'm not sure,' said Taryn hesitantly.

Now that she had been presented with an opportunity to leave, she was not certain that she wanted to take the final step. Ross had indicated that she would not be needed when the children went to school, but surely, since he had paid her fare to come here, she would have to fall in with his wishes?

'I should have to ask Ross,' she explained. 'It depends whether he thinks I'm still needed at Silver Ridge, though I must say at the moment I don't feel very necessary, and it would save his paying my fare home if I were to find another post.'

'I don't think that would concern him very much. But once the children go to school, you won't be able to stay, will you? Even if you stayed to help Mrs. Fuller in the house, I hardly think Coral would want another young girl around once they're married.'

Taryn was surprised by the sudden pain that stabbed like a physical blow to her innermost heart.

'You look pale, Taryn, has the walk been too much for you? Let's open this flask of coffee and have our sandwiches here. You look as if you need something.'

She sipped the coffee gratefully. How foolish to feel such concern over whether Ross should marry a person like Coral! What did it matter to her? She disliked Ross anyway, so why be sorry if he was to marry someone with an apparently vain and shallow nature? With his frank opinions of women, he could certainly cope with a wife of that kind. She remembered Mrs. Schroeder saying he deserved someone better because he was so good. Well, he had charmed her too, as Allister had said he charmed all women.

'But not me,' she said aloud.

'What did you say?' asked Mike.

'Nothing,' Taryn replied. 'Do you think that Ross and

Coral intend to marry soon?'

'Sure to,' said Mike, 'if Coral has anything to do with it. I would say she's ordered her wedding dress already. She won't let him slip through her fingers too easily.'

'But they seem to disagree quite a lot.'

'With a man like Ross that all adds to the spice of living. She's letting him run for a while like a hooked trout, but when she knows the time is right, you see she'll reel him in. The children cramp her style. That's why she went away for a while, I would say. But look how soon he went running off after her to Durban.'

'He said he went on business.'

'Combining it with pleasure. You just see, he'll be off again soon.'

That same evening Allister took the three children to the drive-in cinema in the little town that was a few miles away. Taryn refused his invitation, pleading weariness after her walk. The drive-in was a cinema show in the open air, and one sat in one's car with a soundbox attached to the window to convey the dialogue. Just before they were to go, Mrs. Fuller came into the living-room.

'Mr. Trent, do you think I could possibly get a lift with Mr. Harding into town? I want to see my sister who's just been to visit my mother. She'll have news of her.'

'Certainly, Mrs. Fuller, do go by all means.'

'The only thing is I haven't had time to prepare the dinner yet and I don't know whether . . .'

'I'm sure for once Taryn can cope. She made me an excellent omelette last night.'

'I'm very glad to hear it,' said Mrs. Fuller, flashing a look of dislike at Taryn. 'If I'd known you were returning last night, Mr. Trent, I would have left something to keep hot.'

'I managed very well with Taryn's cooking,' Ross smiled.

Oh, Ross, please don't make it worse, Taryn pleaded silently. Can't you see that whatever you say about me to Mrs. Fuller it will be the wrong thing?

The house seemed very quiet when the children had piled

into Allister's little car and gone laughing and shouting down the valley road, with a disapproving Mrs. Fuller sitting bolt upright in their midst. Taryn was standing in the front porch where she had gone to reassure herself that Adrian was warmly clad, and she became aware that Ross had come up silently behind her. The last golden light was fading on the far mountains and in the cobalt blue sky a few stars were becoming brighter with the deepening darkness.

'Have you noticed how the stars look much nearer to earth here than they ever do in a city?' asked Ross.

'And the sky is deeper blue,' said Taryn.

The air was crisp and clear, and above the noise of the busy stream a curlew called its plaintive sad cry. Taryn shivered in her light dress and Ross put his arm in hers and drew her into the house, shutting the door. He put a match to the fire and she stood there hesitating, still feeling the warmth of his touch on her cold skin. He looked up from his task quite unaware of the effect he had on her, not knowing that when he had taken her arm she had had to resist a foolish impulse to turn and put her hand to his face and run her fingers through the lively brown hair that seemed as if it had an electricity of its own. Discarding these nonsensical thoughts, she said in a determined manner, 'Is there anything you would prefer to eat for dinner?'

He grinned in a teasing way.

'If I can't have Lobster Thermidor, since there are no live lobsters on the premises, how about Tournedos Chasseur? I always go for that.'

He laughed at her blank, panic-stricken expression.

'In other words, my dear Taryn with the huge brown eyes, steak. We shall both go to the kitchen and I shall give you a lesson in Cordon Bleu cooking. You'll be surprised and lost in admiration when you see how accomplished I am. But first a visit to the cellar is indicated.'

What he called his cellar was a kind of hidey-hole under the stairs, cool and dry, where he kept an assortment of good wines. He emerged with a slim bottle and hustled her into the kitchen, where he demanded the ice bucket.

'Moet et Chandon,' he informed her. 'I always like an excuse to drink it.'

'I'm afraid it will be wasted on me.' Taryn protested.

'If it is, you must make a great effort and not tell me,' he warned her as he demanded where Mrs. Fuller kept the tall thin champagne glasses. 'We threw away all the old flat ones,' he said. 'I like to get the bouquet. Now where's that steak?'

They found three small thick pieces of fillet in the refrigerator.

'I'm sure you have a smaller appetite than I have,' said Ross. 'If not, we'll divide it.'

I would never dare to say I wanted more than one even if I did, thought Taryn.

Ross stood over the stove and issued orders to her.

'Three slices of white bread, and see that it's cut thick. Take the crusts off ... mushrooms, tomato paste ... I'm sure Mrs. Fuller keeps tins in the pantry ... butter, olive oil ... chives and parsley ... in a box on the patio ... Madeira ... you'll find that in the drinks cabinet.'

Taryn felt quite breathless by the time she had assembled all the ingredients he required.

'Now sit down like a good girl and we'll try the champagne. It should be chilled by now. It's not the right thing to drink with fillet, but red wine would be too heavy for you. And remember, Taryn, if you're going to drink champagne it's best to drink nothing else. It makes a good aperitif, don't you think?'

They sat at the kitchen bench on two stools that he had drawn up together. As she took her first sip, he looked at her intently and smiled as he saw her small grimace of shock at the chilled unexpected flavour of it.

'Drink some more. You won't appreciate the taste until you've got used to it. Shall we eat in the kitchen and outrage Mrs. Fuller?'

'She won't know, because I shall clear up afterwards,' said Taryn.

She found the champagne light and refreshing but drank it cautiously, while Ross proceeded to cook and at the same time give her a running commentary upon what he was doing. She was amused, surprised and rather touched to see him in a domestic rôle, but on the other hand she felt guilty that she was leaving it to him. One thing was certain – Mrs. Fuller must never know that he had cooked his own dinner.

Instructed by him, she made a French salad to accompany the main dish and they ate the steak piping hot served from the pan on to the fried bread and covered by the delectable sauce. Again Ross watched her as she took her first mouthful. She felt self-conscious, sensing the intent stare of those dark blue eyes, but she forgot about this as her taste buds awoke to the really wonderful taste of his meal.

'It's fantastic!' she declared.

He smiled triumphantly.

'For your information, Taryn, I do everything well.'

'Glorious Mr. Toad,' she smiled.

'What was that?'

'It's from a book I'm reading to Adrian. Mr. Toad of Toad Hall says he can do everything well and he tells everyone so.'

'He sounds an animal after my own heart. Does he come out on top in the end?'

'Yes,' Taryn admitted a bit reluctantly, 'but only after a lot of chastening experiences.'

'What a shame! And is he chastened?'

'No,' said Taryn. 'Not really.'

And nothing would ever make you lose your pride and your downright arrogance, she thought to herself. I can think of you in future as Mr. Toad. And yet in the book Toad is very appealing. One can't deny his charm. And the same goes for Ross.

'He gets his own way all the time,' she murmured aloud.

'That's what I like to hear,' said Ross, smiling at her. 'Have some more champagne.'

They took their coffee into the living-room, where by now there was a glowing log fire. Ross lit a few lamps, but the rest of the room remained shadowy and the soft golden glow around the fireplace gave the room an atmosphere of comfort and homeliness despite its luxurious furnishings. The record player had been left open and Ross put on a record, a dreamy tune that did not disturb the tranquil atmosphere.

'We have enough pop music with the children around, don't you agree?'

Taryn made herself busy with the coffee percolater. She wished they were still in the kitchen with its bright lights and practical atmosphere. Ross seemed to have dropped his teasing conversation and was sitting looking into the fire as if he saw something there that pleased him.

'Thanks for the dinner, Taryn,' he said.

'But it was you who cooked it.'

'Well, perhaps I should say thanks for your company. Sometimes it's fun to do something unexpected and to turn one's hand to cooking instead of always eating out and going to night clubs.'

'I have no experience of that, so I can't say whether I should like it or not.'

'Really? Coral is never happier than when she's found some new place that's fashionable. I thought most women were like that, given the chance.'

'I suppose I would enjoy these things. It's just that I've never done them.'

'How did you learn to dance, because you seemed to be doing pretty well with Allister when I came in last night?'

Why need he remind me of that? thought Taryn. She was feeling relaxed and happy and did not want to think of anything beyond the fact that she was sitting with Ross in his home beside the fire enjoying his company and not being disturbed by doubts and fears as she usually was.

'We used to dance at school. I didn't mean to imply that I'd never had any pleasures at all. On the whole I had a very happy girlhood, in spite of the fact that my parents died when I was too young to understand properly. My grandparents were wonderful to me. It was only during the last couple of years that they became ill and my life was difficult.'

She felt she was saying too much. Maybe the champagne

talking? She must not bore him as much as she thought she had done that day when they had had lunch together. The record player was throbbing out a livelier tune now, one that set the feet tapping.

'Would you care to dance now?' asked Ross.

'If you want to.'

'That's a cool answer,' he said, but at once was beside her, holding both her hands and pulling her to her feet. He whipped away the rug and they stood for a moment on the polished floor, swaying in time to the catchy beat. Then his arms were around her and they were whirling and turning in such harmony that they seemed to be one person.

'They taught you well at this school,' was all he said.

But then the music changed and became slower, more romantic. A singer took up the tune, his voice expressing love and desire and exquisite sadness. Take what's offered, said the singing, because love is an illusion that is soon gone. Taryn felt herself swept up in an emotion she had never felt before.

How foolish she had been to start dancing with Ross, and from such a small thing to feel such terrible sadness. For this little time, they were so much in harmony that she belonged to Ross and Ross to her. But once the haunting tune was over, there would be no more meaning to this close intimacy of two people held in each other's arms, held in a bond of emotion simply inspired by a strain of music.

But when the song ended, he still stood with Taryn held firmly in his arms. Then he put his hand under her chin and turned her face upwards to meet his lips. Her murmured protest was stifled almost at once, for he was kissing her not as Allister had done, flirtatiously, playfully, but like a man who had long thirsted and had come now upon a fountain that he had seen from far off, a fountain of pure clear water that he wished to have entirely for his own.

When it was over, they stood looking at each other, and for a moment Taryn could have sworn that Ross was as shaken as she was. But he put her aside and shook his head as if dispelling a dream.

'There you are, Taryn. Didn't I tell you I do everything well?'

So that was all it had meant to him! He was simply showing her that he could be more romantic than Allister. In a subtle way he had got his revenge for the annoyance he had felt over the scene last night. His exultant smile told her so.

She was trembling, she thought, with anger.

'You may be very pleased with yourself, Ross, but I assure you you haven't impressed me. Thank you for the meal, but the rest of the evening has been five minutes too long. Whether you like it or not, I've had enough of your company. I'm going to bed.'

CHAPTER SEVEN

TARYN lay awake until after the children had come in and settled down. Then her sleep was troubled by restless dreams. Several times she opened her eyes and, staring into the velvety blackness, felt bitter regret that she had allowed herself to be led into such a situation.

For Ross had done it deliberately, she felt sure of that. He had seized the opportunity of being alone with her and twisted it to his own purposes. He was a man who took pride in making an impression, and evidently he had decided to charm her and show her he was more attractive than Allister.

And he had, oh yes, he had. There was no doubt that he could create in her a feeling that she had never experienced before. When she was with him, she felt twice as alive, twice as happy, as she had ever been in all her life. But she must not feel like that. It had no relation to her own rather humdrum existence. He belonged to a world totally alien to hers, a world of high living, of wealth and sophistication. He belonged to Coral. And the scene last night must have given him some amusement. He had probably forgotten about it already. But she felt she could never forget – although she would have to do her best to erase it from her memory for ever.

She dreaded meeting Ross, seeing those dark blue eyes, their smiling expression, hearing the casual greeting over the breakfast table. But she was spared that. When she came downstairs with Adrian chattering at her side about the cowboy film they had seen last night, Mrs. Fuller informed her that Ross had gone back to Durban before anyone else was awake.

'He didn't even stay for breakfast,' she said in a disgruntled fashion. 'I had hoped to tell him the news my sister gave me, but he just had some coffee that Moses made and told him not to wake anyone else.'

'Did you have bad news?' asked Taryn sympathetically.

'I'm not one to tell everyone my troubles,' said Mrs. Fuller in a tone of voice that seemed to mean, 'It's none of your business.' 'But I can tell you this. I have a migraine coming on. I always get a migraine if I'm worried. I'm very sensitive and highly strung, you see. Have been since I was a girl.'

Taryn could not help reflecting that it was a pity Mrs. Fuller's sensitiveness only seemed to extend as far as herself. She did not seem to mind about hurting other people.

'Wouldn't you like to go and lie down?' she asked. 'I'll take Adrian over to the trout hatchery for a walk. Allister is concentrating on the older ones' coaching today. He told me so, because he wanted me to keep Adrian occupied. If I take him for a walk this morning, you'll be able to have a rest.'

'I suppose you and Moses could manage the lunch,' Mrs. Fuller answered grudgingly. 'I wouldn't leave it to you if Mr. Trent were here. He's very particular about his food, as you know.'

At last, after some further discussion, Taryn managed to persuade Mrs. Fuller to go off to her room and, after deciding there was plenty of food for a cold lunch, she and Adrian set off in the direction of the hatcheries. It would be good to see Mrs. Schroeder again, she thought. Chatting to another person and being sociable would take her mind off thoughts of Ross. They walked along the bridle path with Adrian asking questions and demanding answers all the time. Small lizards slipped over the stones and rock rabbits shouted a harsh warning of their approach. Below them the river was like beaten pewter. She had come to love this country with its air like – yes, like the champagne she had drunk last night. It gave the same crisp exhilaration with every breath she took.

Mrs. Shroeder was delighted to see them.

'I've just made some koeksusters, now you can taste something that's really South African,' she said.

She fed them with the golden plaits deliciously dripping with syrup and they drank coffee. The strong bitter taste counteracted the sweetness of the koeksusters.

'These are super, Mrs. Schroeder,' said Adrian. 'Why can't you make them, Taryn?'

'They look too complicated for me,' said Taryn. 'But Mrs. Schroeder, I'd love to know something about South African cooking. What else can you tell me about? Preferably something simple.'

'Let's see. I'm going to make a bobotie for lunch, so you can watch me and then maybe you'll be able to try it. That is, if Mrs. Fuller ever allows you near the kitchen.'

Adrian went out to the hatcheries to watch the fish, but Taryn concentrated on her hostess's preparations for lunch. She had begged a pencil and paper from her and she wrote down all the ingredients and the method of making the meal.

'A lot of our recipes come from the early days at the Cape when the Malay slaves brought their dishes from their homeland. This one has minced meat, onion and curry powder, topped by a mixture of milk and eggs. It's improved by putting a couple of lemon leaves on the top and you can use almonds in it if you have them. Serve it with yellow rice, that is, rice cooked with sugar, salt, a knob of butter, a handful of raisins and a teaspoon of borrie – that's what you call turmeric. You can see it's very simple.'

Taryn was delighted. 'Now I have had my first lesson, can I come for some more?' she asked.

'Certainly, my dear. Next time I shall show you how to make melktert. Then there's tomato bredie and vetkoekies. We'll make you into a South African yet, you'll see!'

Mrs. Schroeder's friendliness was a balm to Taryn's wounded heart. She was so glad she had come here and spent her time doing something practical instead of thinking of Ross. Yet on the way back her thoughts flew to him like homing doves. What was he doing now? Was he having lunch with Coral? Had he phoned her as soon as he reached Durban? It seemed very likely. She knew she was foolish to let him dominate her thoughts. When she thought about it sensibly, she was sure that she did not really like him. The feeling she had had on the few occasions when she had been alone with him was unreal, like a lovely firework scattering its excitement for a little while only to die and be consumed to ashes in the cold light of dawn.

She was kept busy during the next few days. Ross stayed in Durban, and Mrs. Fuller took to her bed for most of the time, leaving the housekeeping to Taryn. It was odd that she was willing to do this, but there was no Ross to impress with her devotion to duty. Taryn managed as best she could. The pantry was very well supplied and the freezer full of different cuts of meat and plenty of vegetables. Moses and his brother were willing and useful with the laundry and the rough work.

Taryn began for the first time to enjoy the household tasks with only distant criticism from Mrs. Fuller. Allister did not help much, but he was good company and seemed to have forgotten his inclination to flirt with Melinda. Taryn watched carefully and saw no sign of this. She was lulled into a secure, almost peaceful feeling. Of course Mrs. Fuller was irritating, implying all the time that Taryn could not possibly be keeping things in order, but she tried to ignore this and to keep the children happy.

Three days had passed with no message from Ross, and Taryn began to feel she had dreamed the events of that last evening. During the afternoon Mike came by in his truck and walked up to where she was sitting on the verandah with Melinda.

'Hello, Taryn, I wondered whether I could persuade you to come to the camp tonight. There's going to be a bit of a do, a film show and perhaps some dancing and supper.'

Taryn hesitated. 'I'm not sure. Do you mean to include the children?'

Melinda spoke up as Mike looked embarrassed.

'Of course he doesn't, Taryn. He just means you. Go on, be a devil for a change and have a night out. She's been slaving away all week because Mrs. Fuller has had one of her migraines. They last for days when Ross is away.'

Mike stood there, a hopeful smile on his craggy freckled face, his red hair standing up in a bush of unruly waves. The thought of going out and having some distraction was tempting. Each evening since Ross had gone, Taryn had sat late by the fire and relived the events of that last night. And this was very foolish, she knew.

'Very well,' she said. 'I'd like to come. Will you be all right, Melinda? I'll leave some supper ready in the oven.'

'We aren't babies,' said Melinda scornfully. 'You go, Taryn. You never go out.'

'I'll call for you at eight,' Mike promised. 'It's informal, of course.'

Just as well, thought Taryn, surveying her scanty wardrobe. It would have to be the pale apricot dress again. She had a light cream shawl that she could wear if the evening became cold. The party was in the Chief Ranger's house and the crowd that had gathered there seemed a friendly bunch. Mike was obviously popular and came in for some backchat as he introduced her around. Supper was in the form of a barbecue, but she noticed that here they called it a braaivleis.

Someone started the record player and soon they were dancing, the rugs and furniture pushed aside. Up to now Taryn had enjoyed the evening, but now she found that the music and dancing, gay as it sounded, brought back a feeling of terrible sadness. She tried to laugh and chat, but all the time she was aware that she was harking back in her mind to that other evening when she had danced alone with Ross. Why was she such a fool? Why could she not enjoy the company of Mike and all these pleasant people? If she took that job that Mike had said might be available, she knew that she could get on very well with them. They did not make her feel uncomfortable or awkward. Mike was rugged and simple and his kind eyes would never make her heart turn somersaults so that she felt she could hardly breathe.

She would have been glad of some excuse to go, but someone decided to show a film on wild life and for a while she lost herself in this. It took quite a time and when they started back in the truck it was almost midnight. Mike drove carefully and steadily over the moonlit track. A silver-backed jackal paused in his investigations of an anthill, then hurried on, looking like a pretty dog. Two porcupines lumbered across the road, and an owl flew, soft as a cloud, into the lights and then away. The mountains showed craggy and black against a sky of deepest blue.

'I didn't mean to stay so long,' said Taryn. 'I hope everything is all right at Silver Ridge.'

'You shouldn't worry so much. Those children are quite capable of looking after themselves, and what's more, Mrs. Fuller and Allister are there, aren't they?'

'Yes, but all the same, I've never left them before.'

'Relax. Ross isn't such a tyrant that he would expect you to stay in the whole time, is he?'

'No-o,' said Taryn doubtfully.

'It's time you left and came to work for me,' said Mike. 'Don't you think it would suit you much better? You wouldn't be a slave to those children, not to mention Ross Trent.'

'Don't say that, Mike, I'm certainly not his slave.'

She said this so vehemently that Mike gave her a surprised look.

'Hold on, I didn't mean to offend you. I only mean that a man like him seems to expect everyone to bow down and worship him.'

'He doesn't do anything of the sort. How can you say such a thing?'

Mike looked quite hurt and Taryn herself realized how unreasonable she was being. It seemed that she herself could criticize Ross, but she was indignant if anyone else did. How stupid could she be?

They drove the last few miles in silence and she felt guilty that she had been hard on Mike after he had taken the trouble to give her a pleasant evening. They came within sight of the house and she could see that from a distance the thatched roof shone like silver and the white walls looked luminous. Below the valley was all in shadow, but the whole homestead and its surroundings glittered in the unearthly light.

'Now you can see why it's called Silver Ridge,' said Mike.

'Yes,' she answered, glad to have something to talk about. 'It looks heavenly in this light, doesn't it?'

But as they drew nearer she was startled to see the lights

blazing from every window.

The children must have forgotten to turn them off, she thought. But no, there in front of the house was the grey Mercedes.

'Ross has come back!' she exclaimed.

'What of it?' asked Mike. 'Taryn, for heaven's sake, anyone would think he was your husband and you had been on some illicit jaunt. I'll come and explain to him if you like.'

'No, don't do that. It will look silly. Of course it's all right. I was just startled. I wasn't expecting he would be home.'

'So here you are,' Ross said sharply with no other greeting. 'Where the devil have you been, Taryn?'

She was puzzled to see Mrs. Fuller standing in the living room in a blue dressing gown, her grey hair down her back in a plait.

'I've been to the camp,' said Taryn. 'Mrs. Fuller knew where I was. Why, whatever's the matter? Is something wrong with Adrian? And where's Melinda?'

'You may well ask,' said Ross grimly. He was frowning and looked quite different from the smiling man who had haunted her dreams.

'It seems that Melinda has gone off to the Mountain Inn to some dance with Allister – that is, if they've arrived there in one piece. I hate to think of Allister's driving on those hairpin bends at night. Didn't you know they were going?'

'Of course not. I would have done my best to dissuade them if I had.'

'I thought Melinda was safe in your care. I never dreamed of her going off with Allister, stupid young fool that he is. I thought it was you he fancied. But Mrs. Fuller tells me Mike called for you quite early. Did they decide to go after that?'

Mrs. Fuller spoke in a self-righteous manner.

'I really didn't know what to say to them, Mr. Trent. You could have knocked me down with a feather when they said they were going out together. But I hardly thought it was my place to object, and Miss Bartlett had gone off to the camp. I did think it was hard, seeing I've been suffering from my migraine for days, that I should be left in charge of the two boys, but what could I do?'

'Yes, yes, I can see that,' Ross said impatiently. 'You'd better get to bed, Mrs. Fuller. You've had enough upset for one night. We shall wait up for Melinda and Allister. And I'll have something to say to that young man when he arrives. He should know better than to take such a young girl up to a place like the Inn where there's quite a lot of drinking in the evening. They'd have to lie about her age to get served there.'

Mrs. Fuller departed up to bed and Taryn was left alone with Ross.

'I'm so sorry, Ross,' she said. 'I hesitated about going out, but Melinda assured me that it would be all right. This must have been a sudden impulse on their part. I really don't think any harm can come of it.'

Ross's expression was grim.

'You know from your own experience, or should do, that Allister is a bit of a philanderer. And Melinda is only fifteen and very attractive. She should be at school, not running round the countryside at night with a young man who's too self-centred and sure of his own charm.'

'I don't know why you're worrying so much, Ross. There's nothing wrong with Melinda. She's just a bit too anxious to grow up. And Allister is trustworthy, I'm sure.'

'Do you think so? No man is really trustworthy with an attractive young woman, Taryn. You should know that.'

Was he referring to the episode of the other evening? All this time she had been standing still while he strode up and down like an agitated panther, but now as he came near her she swayed and he caught her arm and looked closely at her face.

'What is it, Taryn? You look dead on your feet. There are black shadows under those huge eyes of yours and you're like a small ghost. Go up to bed. I'll wait up for Allister and Melinda, and believe me, I'll have something to say to them for causing this upset!'

His tone of voice was such that Taryn felt she had to

obey. And reluctantly she made her way to the stairs.

'Please don't be too hard on them,' she pleaded. 'I feel it's partly my fault for leaving them.'

'Of course it is,' Ross snapped. 'No doubt about it. I needed someone responsible and middle-aged, but I kept you on against my better judgement. However, we shall have to reconsider some other arrangement soon. Meanwhile go to bed and leave me to deal with this.'

She was still awake when she heard the car coming up the road. She heard laughter and happy voices suddenly stilled when they were confronted by Ross. He must have sent Melinda upstairs almost immediately, but Taryn could not bring herself to get up and see her. She was afraid Melinda would be too quick to detect the traces of tears on her face.

Next morning, Allister and Melinda seemed none the worse for Ross's anger. His displeasure seemed to have slipped off them like the proverbial water off a duck's back.

'Coo, that was a bit of bad luck, wasn't it?' Allister said to Taryn. 'We thought we were quite safe with you gone and Ross away. He certainly came the heavy-handed guardian. Lucky I'd had a couple of drinks that blurred the impact of his wrath.'

'It was a foolish thing to do,' Taryn told him.

'You too . . . but of course I suppose you came in for a bit of trouble. Sorry about that, Taryn.'

'It couldn't be helped. I suppose I shouldn't have gone out.'

'I suspect the old girl made it worse. Trust her! Anyhow, cheer up. Things could be worse. I doubt whether either of us is going to be attached to our jobs for very long. We may as well cling to them for as long as we can. We'll soon be out in the cold when the kids go to school.'

I don't know whether I want to cling to mine, thought Taryn. I think I'd better approach Mike about the job he spoke of. He seemed quite keen I should apply. What's the use of staying on here? Ross thoroughly disapproves of me. That kiss and the happiness I felt the other evening was simply because he wanted to prove something, that he could be more attractive than Allister, I suppose. But there was nothing personal about it, and the sooner I get away from this house the better. I'll try to get an opportunity to tell Mike I want to be considered for that work at the camp.

She had not seen Ross this morning, as he had gone off early to see his forestry plantation. Allister seemed to be very diligently occupied, trying to make up, she supposed, for the bad impression he had created the night before. Taryn spoke to him, mentioning that she thought of going to the camp to see Mike.

'What's he got that I haven't got?' Allister asked. Melinda looked annoyed. 'I didn't realize Mike had such fatal charm,' she said.

Taryn merely smiled and was not offended. She realized that Melinda was taking out her annoyance from the night before, spitting and scratching at anything near like a small blue-eyed kitten. Mrs. Fuller was more pleasant than usual and Taryn was surprised. 'It will do you good to get out,' she said. 'You're looking pale.'

'I won't be long,' said Taryn. 'I want to go while the children are occupied. I'll be back soon. I just want to go to the camp.'

'Stay as long as you like. After all, it's not the same as at night. Nothing can happen to worry Mr. Trent this morning.'

'You knew where I was,' said Taryn, stung to retort. 'If you were worried about them, you could have phoned the camp.'

'I'm not one to interfere,' said Mrs. Fuller smugly.

Walking along the path to the camp. Taryn could not appreciate the beauty of her surroundings. She felt thoroughly exasperated. Everything she did seemed to be wrong. An innocent outing with Mike had turned out to be an absolute disaster. She felt she must get out of her present situation as soon as possible.

When she arrived at the camp, she found that Mike had gone up the hillside to supervise some work, but the warden assured her that she would easily find him and that it was not far, but it took longer than she had intended and was quite tiring uphill walking before they met. He was delighted to see her and made her sit down and share his coffee and sandwiches. She did not confide in him about Ross's anger of the night before, but he must have guessed there was a good reason why she had sought him out.

'I'll speak to the warden,' he promised. 'And if he's agreeable, you can start as soon as you can be free from this job. When do you think that will be?'

'I don't know. I shall speak to Ross today. I don't think he'll regret it if I leave. Oh, Mike, everything always seems to go wrong that I do. I hope I'm not going to let you down in this post.'

She looked so woebegone that he put his arm around her and gave her a squeeze.

'Not to worry. I'm quite sure I can make you happy.'

He looked at her significantly and she wished he had not put it like that. Did he think . . .? But no, he was merely trying to help her. And she would be happy. She felt defeated by the whole set-up at Silver Ridge and she must admit it to Ross and call it a day. The children were her only reason for staying and they would be going soon. They didn't really need her anyway. Melinda certainly would rather she was not there to interfere.

Now she had made her decision, she felt calmer and, walking back with the fragrances of wild grasses around her, and the background of mountains under a tranquil sky, she was glad she would be staying here but in much less luxurious surroundings. Mike had told her she would have a small thatched hut to herself, furnished with a simple bed, table and chairs, and she felt sure she could be content there without all the luxury to which she had never previously been accustomed.

She need not see Ross again after she had left, since he never came to the camp and, once the children had gone to school, his visits to Silver Ridge would be fleeting. And Taryn would be rid of the emotions that brought such conflict to her mind and heart. He was too hard, too arrogant, too difficult altogether, and — yes, too self-opinionated.

She would be happy to be rid of his disturbing presence.

She was feeling almost peaceful now as she approached the house. The sun was sparkling on the waters of the pool where the wild ducks and terns made widening ripples as they splashed and swam. It all looked so lovely. Thank goodness we've got over the drama of last night, she thought. I hope I can pass the last few days here with no more upsets.

Melinda met her at the door. Her eyes were wide.

'Taryn, oh, thank goodness you've come! I thought you were going to stay for lunch and I don't know what I would have done if you had.'

'Why, whatever is the matter?'

'Mrs. Fuller has packed her bags and gone. A car came to fetch her. She says her sister sent for her to go to her mother, but I don't believe her. She must have arranged it before. I think she's just got the huff about having a crowd here. And Ross's manager just phoned from Durban to say that two important American people are coming for lunch, a man and his wife. They're on their way in a small plane and they want to be met at the air-strip. What are we to do? Ross will expect a decent lunch for these Americans. He likes to make a good impression.'

'I suppose we can get a message through to Ross at the plantation and Allister could go to meet them. He'd better start off immediately.'

'But what about lunch?' Melinda asked.

'I shall have to do what I can. Meanwhile you phone Ross. But don't mention that Mrs. Fuller has gone. Just tell him about the Americans coming.'

Taryn went into the kitchen where Moses was belatedly washing up the breakfast things. He was rather scared of using the dishwasher on his own. Taryn wondered what she could do. It was all very well catering for the family, but a different thing to serve an important lunch. She racked her brains, but felt so panic-stricken that ideas flew in and out of her brain and she could not decide what would be best. She was still gazing desperately into the freezer when Melinda came back.

'He says I'm to tell Mrs. Fuller that she must prepare something a bit special and out of the ordinary. So what do we do?' The phone rang sharply. 'You answer it this time, Taryn. I'm sure to say the wrong thing if it's Ross again.'

But it was Mrs. Schroeder. Her pleasant voice came over the line, asking, 'When are you coming to have another cookery demonstration?'

'Heavens, Mrs. Schroeder, you are an angel to phone. You've given me an idea. Tell me properly over again how to make that South African bobotie.' And Taryn explained her predicament.

'You poor child! I wish I could come up and help you, but I can't come right now. However, I tell you what I'll do. I have some fresh koeksusters that you can serve with coffee, and some homemade pickled peaches to go with your bobotie. I'll ask my husband to drop them off at your place – he's going to the camp very shortly. And I can send a few small fresh trout if that would help. I'll roll them in oatmeal and all you'll have to do is fry them in oil and butter. That will do for your first course.'

'Oh, Mrs. Schroeder, I can't thank you enough!'

Once she had decided what to do, it seemed no trouble at all to cook the lunch. Taryn flew around the kitchen with Melinda being most helpful for a change.

'It's heavenly to be without Mrs. Fuller,' Melinda rejoiced. 'I hope she never comes back.'

When Ross strode in a little before one o'clock, everything was under control. Allister had gone to the air-strip to collect the visitors, and all Ross had to do was to choose and chill the wine. There was hardly time to explain about Mrs. Fuller. Taryn and Melinda were too busy for that.

'I might have known something like this was on the go,' was all Ross said when he heard. 'She told me her mother was ailing, but she has been so for some time. I think she was glad of an excuse to leave us all. I was a bit hopeful, I suppose, to think she would take kindly to a houseful of people when she's been used to an easy time for so long. She seemed an efficient person until I inflicted a family on her.'

And me too, thought Taryn. I was certainly not very popular with her. But Taryn was too busy with the lunch preparations to pay much heed to these thoughts. Melinda set the table on the patio that overlooked the lovely view of blue mountains, and they chose a set of cutlery with wooden handles, a handwoven set of mats in rustic colours of mingled browns, handmade pottery plates, and Melinda did a hasty arrangement of wild grasses that she found near the pool.

Meanwhile Taryn was making good progress with her cooking, and by the time the American couple arrived the trout were brown and crisp, done to a turn, the bobotie was baking successfully, and the rice was yellow and appetizing, studded wth plump raisins. Melinda prepared the cheeseboard on a wooden platter and Taryn made a green salad.

'You've done wonders,' said Ross, jubilantly, to the two of them, as he came into the kitchen to fetch the wine.

The Americans, a pleasant couple from Atlanta, Georgia, seemed charmed with the informality of the meal that followed.

'I declare,' said Mrs. Houzet, 'I've wanted to taste a real South African meal since we got here, and all they offer us at these five-star hotels is Continental dishes you get all over the world. Isn't this something, Hiram, to be sitting outside on a patio looking at this gorgeous view and eating real tasty food? And what clever little girls you have, Mr. Trent, to produce a meal like this. I really must congratulate them.'

Mrs. Hiram B. Houzet seemed a bit confused about the relationship between Ross and his large family – and no wonder, thought Taryn. Ross was at his best, full of sparkling vitality and charm, giving the couple the information they wanted about the country and in a subtle way about his business.

When Ross had taken the guests off to the airstrip, Taryn and Melinda collapsed into the long reclining chairs that were on the patio.

'Thank goodness, Moses has cleared away,' said Melinda. 'Allister, be an angel and bring me a Coke.'

Up to now, Taryn had had no time to think about Mrs. Fuller's sudden departure and the implications as far as she was concerned. But now, though she was physically tired with the unaccustomed effort, her mind buzzed with questions. What was to happen if Mrs. Fuller intended to stay away for a long time? Taryn felt she could not let Ross down. She would have to stay. But Mike wanted her to take his job almost immediately. She could not keep him waiting around for her decision.

When Ross arrived back, he was very cheerful.

'You girls really did wonders. I should never have thought it possible in the time.'

'We owed a lot to Mrs. Schroeder,' Taryn told him. 'She helped out with the trout and the koeksusters, and if it hadn't been for her, I should never have known how to make a bobotie.'

'Nevertheless, it was an inspiration to give them a South African meal. They were charmed. We must remember that next time we have overseas visitors for lunch here.'

But will there be a next time for me? thought Taryn.

CHAPTER EIGHT

IT was two weeks later and Mike and Taryn were sitting on the slope of a hill not far from the house. They had met because she had phoned to say she would like to see him during the afternoon. Below them a herd of eland grazed peacefully like so many cattle, their gentle heads contrasting strangely with the huge bulk of their bodies.

'I'm very disappointed,' Mike was saying.

A troubled frown made his usually cheerful expression gloomy.

'I'm so sorry, Mike. I think I would have liked the job, but you can see how it is for me.'

'I can see that in spite of your denials, Ross has made a slave of you just like he does of anyone else he employs.'

'That's not fair! It's Melinda I'm thinking about, not Ross.'

'I wonder,' said Mike.

Taryn tried to explain again.

'At first I couldn't let Ross down because Mrs. Fuller had gone. We didn't know whether she'd be back or not, but finally she sent a message to say she didn't intend to return.'

'Yes, I understood all that,' said Mike impatiently. 'And I was willing to try to delay this job for you somehow until things were sorted out. But now that Ross has engaged Mrs. Schroeder's sister as housekeeper, I don't see why you feel obliged to stay any longer.'

'Oh, Mike, I've explained it all. You don't seem to understand that because Ross brought me out here, I feel I have to consider his wishes first. I thought he didn't need me any more and would be glad to be rid of me, but now he says he's arranged that Melinda should go to a coaching school in Durban before going to boarding school and he wants me to stay in the penthouse with her. She can't very well stay there alone.'

'But why does he want her to go to Durban? I thought that was why he'd engaged Allister to coach the three of them.'

'To tell you the truth, this is confidential, Mike, Melinda is getting a bit too attracted to Allister, or so it seems to Ross, so he wants to get her out of the way for a while.'

'So that's it,' said Mike. 'And so you have to sacrifice the chance of an interesting job you were sure you'd like, in surroundings you've said you love, just so that you can be chaperone to Melinda for a few months. Why doesn't he just send her to school now and let her sink or swim?'

'Because he promised their parents he would do it this way. It's no use arguing, Mike, I've told him I'm willing to go to look after the apartment and keep Melinda company.'

'And where will he be?'

'I don't know. Sometimes on business trips, sometimes at Silver Ridge, but sometimes at the flat, I suppose. After all, it is his, Mike.'

'It seems to me he's getting you away from here as well. He likes to keep all his women to himself.'

'That's ridiculous! I'm certainly not one of his women, whatever you may mean by that.'

'I'm sorry, Taryn. I guess I went too far, but I'm pretty cut up about this decision of yours. I thought you liked this part of the world, and I hoped you liked me a bit.'

'I do, Mike, I do.'

She stood up, eager to end the scene, and he rose too, but before she could turn to walk back towards the house, he had put his arms around her.

'Won't this make you stay?' he said, and kissed her firmly on the lips. 'Oh, Taryn, Taryn, don't you know how I feel about you? I thought you understood why I wanted you near.'

'No, Mike, please don't say any more. You'll only be sorry if you do.'

'I meant to lead up to it gradually. I know I haven't much to offer, Taryn, but I thought you could grow to love the country and perhaps me.'

119

'I do like you very much indeed.' He was still holding her inescapably in his arms and the cool wind had not yet erased the warmth of his kiss on her lips. 'Don't make it more difficult for me, Mike, I'm truly sorry I have to let you down.'

'I suppose I was a fool to think I could part you from Ross Trent so easily,' he muttered.

'Don't say that, Mike. You make me angry when you keep implying that there's something between us. Ross cares for Coral, if he cares for anyone but himself. He's my employer and nothing else.'

They had been so absorbed in their conversation that only now did they notice a figure striding up the path.

'Here's your employer himself,' said Mike, his arms dropping to his sides. 'No doubt you would prefer to go home with him.'

He walked away, scarcely greeting Ross as he passed him.

'What have you been saying to Mike?' inquired Ross. 'He doesn't look too pleased. And yet I could have sworn he was kissing you as I came up the hill. Now tell me it's none of my business.'

Taryn did not feel she could reveal to Ross the real reason why Mike was displeased. Since he had asked her to go with Melinda to Durban, she had put out of her mind the thought of taking the job Mike had offered. And she had not realized that Mike had formed such a strong attachment to her – or thought he had. Perhaps it was just as well she was going away. The time in Durban would not be for very long. Ross would presumably be away for most of the time and Coral would see that he was occupied with her when he was there.

'It was just a misunderstanding,' she replied to Ross's question.

'You shouldn't flirt with him. He's a good chap.'

Taryn looked up at him. She could not read the expression of those dark blue eyes that seemed to gaze at her so penetratingly and yet so enigmatically.

'Mike can look after himself,' she said. 'He doesn't need

your protection.'

'But Melinda needs yours,' said Ross. 'Are you sure you're quite happy about taking her to Durban?'

'Of course I am. She's a sweet child. The question is, are you happy for me to take her?'

'I wouldn't have asked you otherwise. I must admit it seems a good idea to get you and Melinda away from that young man. He's a good teacher, but seems unreliable where women are concerned.'

'That's not unusual,' Taryn told him.

Ross threw back his head and laughed.

'You remind me sometimes of a sweet kitten, Taryn. Everything is soft about you, your eyes, your hair, your skin, but I didn't know you could show your claws!'

They began to walk slowly back to the house. The sun was setting, casting shafts of golden light in to the valleys. In spite of the upsetting scene with Mike, Taryn felt happy. How was it that, however Ross annoyed her, she could feel this simple contentment just walking by his side? It would soon be over. In a couple of days' time, she was to go to Durban, and she did not suppose she would ever come back to Silver Ridge. If she did, she would come as a stranger. But had she ever been anything else?

In a few days' time, Taryn and Melinda were installed in the penthouse in Durban. Ross had sent a car to fetch them from Silver Ridge as he had business elsewhere, but this was an advantage in a way because they could explore their surroundings with the maximum of curiosity. Melinda, who at first had been quiet and a little sulky at having to leave Allister, now had a revival of good spirits and waltzed around the huge living room declaring, 'Don't you think this was a good move, Taryn? Here we are in this fantastic place with no one to disturb us. I'm off men, for a while at any rate. It will be fabulous to have a bit of freedom on our own.'

'It hasn't taken you long to be off men, Melinda. And as to being free, you've come here to go to coaching school. Don't forget that.'

'Don't be so crushing, Taryn. It's so lovely here and we'll have the weekends free. And oh, look, there's a swimming pool outside on the patio! We'll be able to catch a tan, and it's so high no one can overlook us.'

Melinda's high spirits were infectious. It really was a beautiful place to live in, almost too beautiful. It looked as if it had been furnished just for show, and Taryn supposed that this was so. Silver Ridge was the place that Ross liked best. This was his place for living in town, his bachelor pad, furnished to impress his visitors from overseas and, she supposed, his girl-friends.

Everything was pale gold, the carpet that covered the whole floor, the period chairs covered in velvet, the leather top of the antique desk in amber with gold tooling, and the floor-length curtains that swept across the whole of one wall and framed a view of towering buildings far below, and beyond that the sea and the harbour mouth. The touches of other colours were in the glowing Persian rugs and the velvet cushions in jewel colours, jade and ruby and topaz.

The flat was serviced, cleaned by the staff each morning. Melinda was keen to eat in the restaurant downstairs, but Taryn felt she must earn her keep by providing dinner when Melinda came from the tutorial college. The first few days passed pleasantly. Melinda caught a bus each morning, came home in the afternoon and did her homework at night. Ross had suggested that it would be useful if Taryn took driving lessons, so she spent the morning in this manner and then sometimes went to the beach with Melinda or otherwise swam in the pool on the penthouse roof. After a few days they both looked very brown and attractive.

One afternoon Melinda came home from the teaching college and said, looking a bit embarrassed, 'Taryn, do you mind if I go swimming this afternoon with some girls from the college? They keep asking me and I think it's unfriendly to keep saying no.'

Taryn had meant to suggest they should stay at home and swim there, as she wanted to prepare a casserole for dinner.

'You won't be late, will you?'

'You won't be late, or eat too much ice-cream or talk to any boys,' Melinda mocked her. 'Truly, Taryn, anyone would think I was six years old, the way you and Ross carry on!'

'It might be better if you were,' said Taryn.

'Ross has made you into a mother hen about me. I'm not going to go wild just because I go the beach with a few girls. You're so careful of me, you make me want to break out sometimes.'

'I'm sorry, Melinda. Of course you can go.'

It was hard on the child, Taryn thought, if she was never to go out with her friends and always be chaperoned by her. Ross had exaggerated ideas on the subject of Melinda's safety. And she herself had been affected by it.

Melinda went off with her bikini under her cotton beach-wrap, and Taryn, after she had set the casserole simmering, decided to have a swim in the pool. She had invested in a tanga, a minute two-piece garment tied at the sides with strings of the same material. She would never have thought of wearing it on the beach, but here it was completely private and they were so high in the air they could not be overlooked. She started swimming, but after a while she floated on the surface, dreamily scanning the sky that seemed a paler blue here in the city than it had been at Silver Ridge.

Every now and again a jet thundered overhead, a trail of white smoke showing behind it as it made for the airport. But apart from that, there were no noises to remind one that there was a flourishing city all around. Of course this was a block of luxury flats built on the ridge, the highest part of the city. Ross seemed to have a passion for having his dwelling on the heights whether in city or country. He was like one of those black eagles needing his own eyrie – yes, he isolated himself from the common herd and he led his own life, coming and going according to his own self-made rules.

'How I miss him,' Taryn said to herself. The thought had crept up on her unawares and she tried to dismiss it. But it was difficult not to dream about the time at Silver Ridge, which now, looking back, seemed to have given her so much happiness in spite of all the troubles. Here, even though the surroundings were luxurious and Melinda seemed meek and amiable, she herself felt as if she were just marking time. What was to happen next? Where could she go after this?

She heard a gay whistle from the side of the pool.

'So this is where you are, Taryn. You look a lovely sight for a tired business man. Mind if I join you?'

Ross vanished so quickly that she almost felt she had dreamed his voice because she had been thinking about him so earnestly, but in a few moments he was back in a dark blue costume, and diving into the pool, came up at her side, shaking the drops from his curling brown hair.

'I can't boast as scanty a costume as you. Is that a new idea?'

Taryn swam away a few paces, but he followed her.

'I didn't think anyone would be here,' she said. 'It's a new kind of bikini called a tanga. Melinda and I bought them just for this pool so we could tan well. People do wear them on the beach, but we don't.'

'I should think anyone brave enough to wear it on the beach would deserve a medal, and I'm sure the person who invented it does too.'

He caught her by the shoulders and took her chin in his hand.

'Don't look so distressed, Taryn. You look quite beautiful in it. You have a very lovely body – I mean that. No, don't go.' Taryn was swimming away, but he caught her back. 'Why do you like to run away from me? It's a perfectly delightful afternoon, and here we are alone together, the first occasion for a long time. Stay here. Share my pleasure.'

If I had any sense, thought Taryn, I would get out of the pool right now and say I have something urgent to do about cooking dinner, but she was held by his smile, the depth of colour in his dark-fringed eyes, the compelling arm that guided her to the small fountain that spilled its sparkling drops into the pool.

'Stand here,' he commanded, piloting her to the steps beside the water. 'There, I knew this would make a perfect picture. You look like a dryad in a forest pool, with your long wet hair and those huge beseeching eyes. I should like to take your photograph, but I don't trust you not to run away for refuge once I've gone.'

'If I remember correctly,' Taryn said tremulously, 'dryads always had tragic histories, falling in love with unsuitable people and being turned into a tree or foam – or am I thinking of little mermaids?'

'Probably both,' said Ross, laughing. 'Come and improve that honey-coloured skin with a little more sun.'

He led her to where a chaise-longue in bright canvas was placed invitingly near the pool and when he had pushed her gently into the seat he sat close by. Taryn leaned back and closed her eyes. There were dazzling fireworks in the blackness beyond her lids. She felt defenceless against his flattery, for it was only that. He was trying to bind her to him as he tried to attract any woman with whom he had any intimate contact. Why did he torment her? She felt such happiness when he praised her, even though she knew in her heart that what he said was untrue.

'Talking of falling in love with unsuitable people,' said Ross, 'I saw Mike before I left Silver Ridge. If you're interested in that direction, I must warn you that he has a new girl in his office. Quite an attractive person, she seemed. She's the daughter of one of the Parks men, so if she gets on with Mike at least she'll know what she's in for.'

'Are you trying to make me jealous?' asked Taryn.

She opened her eyes and saw Ross looking at her intently.

'Yes, of course, why not? I was curious to note your reaction, but I'm sorry to say that I don't think Mike has much chance with you. You didn't even look cross when I told you about Mike's new assistant.'

'Why should I be?'

'Didn't he offer the job to you first?'

Ross knew altogether too much, thought Taryn.

'As a matter of fact, he did, but I turned it down.'

'So that's why he had a face like thunder the day I met you on the hill above the house. And I thought it was because he'd proposed to you and been refused. Well, we live and learn.'

Taryn did not tell Ross that it had almost been as he said. In any case, that was all over now. When she had to find another job, she would look for one at a distance from Silver Ridge. It would be best to put herself at a safe distance from Ross, where she could not feel thrilled by what she knew was only flattery of the kind he handed out to every woman. And yet, lying here looking at the puffs of white vapour trails left by a jet aircraft, she was stricken with misery when she thought that one of these days that jet might be the one in which she was being carried swiftly away from the life here that she had learned to love.

She felt Ross slide his hand into hers.

'Am I forgiven?'

'For what?' she asked.

'For teasing you about Mike?'

'Don't give it another thought.'

She had more to forgive than that small thing, she pondered. He had not begged to be forgiven because he did not even know that he had brought her out of the chrysalis that had enclosed her for her whole life long, but like a butterfly that had newly acquired wings, she was finding it painful and difficult to get out and fly. Yet a butterfly eventually spread its wings and soared into the air in bright beauty. That was not for her. She was more like a small sea-creature which had outgrown its former shell and now found itself defenceless.

'I feel a new person after that swim,' said Ross. 'Where's Melinda, by the way?'

'She's gone down to the beach with some friends.'

'Have you met them?'

'No, but, Ross, you can't expect her to be satisfied with my company all the time.'

'I must insist that you ask her to bring her friends here so that you can vet them before she goes out with them.'

'Ross, it's very difficult to act as a gaoler. I can't see any harm in her going out with the girl friends she meets at this college. If you put too much restriction on her it will have a bad effect with someone like Melinda.'

'I'd rather be sure than sorry. She's not my daughter, so I feel I can't be too careful.'

'You'd make a good Spanish Don, keeping your daughters in a hacienda, or a pasha with a harem.'

Ross threw back his head and laughed. Drops of water were shaken from his hair and ran shining down his nut-brown skin.

'Heaven preserve me from a harem! I have enough trouble with the small assortment of women I know.'

Melinda, to Taryn's relief, was not at all late. She was delighted to see Ross and flung herself at him, exclaiming, 'What a lovely surprise! And are you staying the night with us? Won't you take us out to dinner? Taryn only has an old casserole. We can use it tomorrow.'

Ross looked a shade embarrassed.

'I'm sorry, Melinda, I have an appointment for tonight. In fact I should be changing now. I'm late already. And I won't be staying here, I'm going to a friend's flat. I didn't think there'd be room for me.'

'Of course there is. You don't think we use your room, do you? Oh, Ross, we haven't seen you for ages. I thought you'd want to be with us.'

Taryn thought it was good to be as young as Melinda and to be able to voice your thoughts without any restraint. She too felt disappointed that his visit was to end so soon. She thought he probably had a date with Coral.

'You're going out with a girl,' Melinda accused him, twining her arms around his neck and smiling up at him, her blue eyes enchanting. 'We're very jealous of all your girl-friends, aren't we, Taryn?'

'Are you, Taryn?' asked Ross.

She shook her head numbly, trying to smile at Melinda's banter.

'We'll arrange an evening out together another time, I promise you. I'll be back again soon. I'm expecting some people from overseas – I'm not sure when to expect them. But you can come too when I entertain them.'

He went off to change, and Taryn, after putting on a cotton dress, went to inspect her casserole. They were sitting down to eat in the kitchen alcove when he came in.

'You look quite gorgeous,' Melinda exclaimed. 'How I wish you were taking us out and that the girls at school could see you!'

It was the first time that Taryn had seen Ross in a dark formal suit, and it certainly complemented his height and good looks.

'I hope Coral appreciates you and dresses to match,' said Melinda slyly.

Ross nodded. 'She usually does,' he said. 'Please, Taryn, come to my room and help me to fasten these cufflinks.'

She followed him into the large room with its wide bed made of a carved wood frame and a head and footboard of black leather. Some interior decorator had been given a free hand with it, she had thought when she first saw it. The room at Silver Ridge was more characteristic of his own taste. This was opulent and impressive, but more like something in a magazine that would be described as a young executive's suite.

She threaded the thin gold cufflinks through the cuffs, fumbling a little and very conscious that his face was inches from her bent head.

'There, I think that's all right,' she said, shaking back her hair.

'You'd better brush me now,' he said, laughing and handing her one of the silver-backed brushes from the table. 'I'd better not go to meet Coral with your long brown hairs on my suit.'

'You're quite safe,' she said, brushing him down. 'There's nothing there.'

'Thank you, Taryn. You're very useful.'

He smiled and dropped a kiss on her cheek. He would have done the same to Melinda, she thought.

After supper, she and Melinda sat on the patio under the stars. It was a lovely, mellow night, not fresh and crisp as it had been in the mountains, but warm and tropical. A golden moon rose over the sea, making a path upon the dark waves. It was a night for romance, for being with one you loved.

'I hope Coral realizes how lucky she is,' said Melinda.

CHAPTER NINE

IN spite of the fact that Melinda seemed to have settled well at the coaching college and that she was rapidly catching up on the syllabus she would have to face when she went to boarding school, Taryn felt uneasy about her. On the surface there seemed nothing wrong. After Ross's visit, trying to comply with his wishes, she had done her best to encourage Melinda to bring her friends to the apartment.

Melinda only brought girls and they spent their afternoons swimming and playing pop music and practising dancing with each other. She said she did not know any boys, or at least that she was not sufficiently interested to bring them around. So although there always seemed to be a lot of giggling and whispering and talk about boys, Taryn had to be contented with this explanation.

'They're awful drips at the college,' Melinda said. 'After Ross and Allister, young boys seem uninteresting.'

'That's all right with me. I don't want to force them on you by any means. I only wondered whether you got tired of only having girls here,' Taryn told her.

'No, I'm quite happy. I wish you wouldn't fuss.'

Melinda went to the beach a great deal, but she said she and her friends did not bother about boys. Perhaps this was true. Taryn hoped so.

The time was going by swiftly now and soon she would have to decide what she would do when Melinda and the others went to school. She would have to look for a job in the city. There would not be another like Mike's offer in the reserve. That chance had gone. One day Ross breezed in unexpectedly saying he had just come from a business trip to Johannesburg.

'I'm taking a party of Americans to a game reserve over the week-end,' he announced. 'Would you and Melinda care to come with us?'

'Whee!' shouted Melinda. 'That will be super!'

'And you, Taryn?'

She nodded. 'Of course I should love it.'

'There are two young men, so I thought they would appreciate a little feminine company. Coral says she can come too.'

Taryn frowned warningly at Melinda whose face had changed its joyful expression, but before she could impress her, she moaned, 'Coral? Oh, must she come?'

'Don't be childish, Melinda. Coral is an attractive addition to any party. I particularly want to impress these young men, so please try to be sensible. You always seem to want to be more grown-up than you are, now here's your opportunity. I don't mean you should be precocious with them, but just be natural and as charming as I know you can be.'

It was a good thing that Ross had added a compliment at the end of his advice, for Melinda was looking hurt and mutinous.

'Oh, all right,' she said. 'But I wish it were just Taryn and me.'

At the start of the week-end, Ross sent a car to fetch Taryn and Melinda, and then they had to call for Coral. She arrived in the foyer of her apartment block wearing a beautifully cut cream slacks suit, the jacket cut in safari style. An emerald green cravat was the exact colour of her eyes and the cream of the suit made a lovely foil for her honey-coloured skin and dark, almost black hair. She motioned to the porter to bring out two cream-coloured suitcases and a vanity case of the same colour. Melinda gazed at these in astonishment.

'But we're only going for the week-end,' she whispered to Taryn.

'Hush, it has nothing to do with us.'

Until they had seen Coral, they had both been feeling rather pleased with themselves, for they had been on a small shopping spree in honour of the occasion and bought themselves new jeans and tops. Melinda's were of faded blue denim with a sleeveless tank top in blue and white, and Taryn was wearing brown cotton slacks with a brown and white striped shirt blouse.

Coral greeted them briefly. She was displeased that Ross had not called for her himself and did not hesitate to say so.

'I can't think why Ross has made such a large party this time,' she complained. 'I've often acted as hostess for him and he's never insisted on bringing anyone else but his business guests.'

'He didn't have us before,' said Melinda. 'We're almost like his family now, aren't we, Taryn?'

'I should say you are, Melinda,' said Coral, before Taryn could think of a suitable reply. 'And of course families always bring their own particular troubles, don't they?'

'Ross doesn't think we're troublesome,' Melinda denied hotly.

'No? All the same, Melinda, I think he'll be very pleased when you and Damon and Adrian are safely at school, and there's no need for further supervision.'

That means me, thought Taryn. She means that she herself will be glad when we've all gone. I suppose she resents the time Ross spends with us. But goodness knows, that's very little.

'That will be quite soon,' she said to Coral placatingly as she saw Melinda's angry expression.

'Will you be going back to England when the children go to school?' asked Coral.

'I'm not sure. I may try to find something else to do.'

'It's nonsense that Ross should be made to feel responsible for you too, and I told him so the other evening. It was generous of him to pay your fare out here, considering that you've had to do so little. You mustn't expect to pick up such a good salary in any other job that you got in Durban, and you would certainly have to work much harder. I think it would be much better if you told Ross you wanted to go home.'

'I shall decide when the time comes,' said Taryn.

Why was Coral so anxious to get rid of her? Perhaps she thought it would be a nuisance to her if Ross kept her for some kind of domestic post. Well, that would not happen.

The young Americans' time was limited, so Ross had decided to save time by flying them all to the game reserve in Zululand in the eight-seater jet plane he used in his business. It was waiting at the Virginia airport that was for private planes only, close to the blue Indian Ocean. Ross was there with the two young Americans, Brad Wallace, a tall, good-looking, athletic type with blond hair and a healthy tan, and Edgar Spencer, a shorter, more rotund man. After sizing up the feminine company, Brad had eyes only for Coral, but Edgar chatted to everyone in a very easy way.

They flew low over the coast, over blue sea with white waves curling upon the small coves edged with wild banana trees, then, going inland, the landscape changed and there were wide expanses of grassland with groups of trees. In what seemed no time at all they were down on to an airstrip and Ross had a small minibus waiting for them to drive them to the Reserve. They were met at the gates by a smiling Zulu guard of huge physique, who took their particulars and waved them on their way.

Now the vehicle had to go slowly, as there was a speed limit, but this was necessary, for otherwise they would have missed seeing the wild life, so cunningly were the animals hidden amongst bush and grass. The high minibus was much better than a car for viewing the landscape, and Melinda was the first to shout to the driver to halt.

'I can't believe it. Look over there on that hill!'

A crowd of giraffes were cropping the green leaves from the trees that were only as tall as themselves. They were so astonishing with their velvety brown patches and small heads above long necks and sloping bodies. There were small ones too like toys, exact replicas of their large parents. Ross produced a pair of powerful fieldglasses, and Taryn admired their gentle small heads.

'Oh, what lovely eyes, so brown and long-lashed!' she exclaimed.

'Like yours,' whispered Ross, leaning forward to take the glasses.

Was it a compliment to have eyes compared to those of a giraffe? Taryn wondered. I suppose it's better than having cowlike eyes, she thought.

As they drove deeper into the reserve towards the place where they were to stay, it was like some large open parkland, grassy with flat-topped thorn trees. Every now and again, antelope moved in dignified pace across the roads. A kudu bull, huge and magnificent, stopped frozen by the sight of the car. It stood with its beautiful spiral horns flung back and stared for a moment with startled eyes, then gave a huge leap and vanished into the bush at the side of the road. Troops of dainty auburn impala sped swiftly along, and warthogs, ludicrous with grey muddy pelts and small curling horns, ran with tails held erect. Zebras, sleek and striped, flashed through the trees like large rocking horses.

'This sure looks like Africa to me,' said Brad.

The rest camp was a large group of white thatched huts within a fenced enclosure. It was set upon a high ridge so that it was possible to look out over miles of country.

The huts were quite basic, with three beds, a table and chairs, a cupboard for the food and a small refrigerator. They had brought their own food, but there were central kitchens where Africans were ready to cook simple meals. The girls were to share one hut and the men another. As soon as they had left the men, Coral began to complain.

'I should have thought Ross could take us to a decent hotel outside the reserve. I didn't realize he expected us to stay in the camp. I thought he was joking when he said so. Good heavens, there isn't anywhere to hang my clothes!'

'But we're only staying until tomorrow, Coral,' said Taryn. 'Surely there's no need to unpack much.'

'I think it's lovely,' said Melinda. 'And Taryn won't even have to cook.'

'Lucky Taryn,' said Coral acidly. 'And where, may I ask, is the bathroom?'

'There's an ablution block next to the kitchen, quite close by.'

Taryn herself was very impressed with the place, the clean bare rooms, the atmosphere of being far away from any town. The wilderness seemed to drowse in the noonday heat, the only sounds the bubbling cooing of doves and the cry of a kestrel hawk. Taryn went to help Ross unpack the tins of food they had brought with them. Together they decided to open a tin of ham and have some salad. They would have a hot meal in the evening.

They sat on canvas chairs under the shade of a flat-topped tree, with cans of beer and cool drinks placed on a table made from a tree trunk. Coral had recovered from her ill humour and was basking in the admiration of the young American, Brad Wallace. Was she making a play for him deliberately to arouse Ross's jealousy? Taryn wondered. But Ross did not seem disturbed. He sat looking relaxed and happy, talking about the game reserves to Edgar and Melinda.

Below them there were bush-covered hills and dark valleys with a river winding its way in silver curves.

'That is the real wilderness,' said Ross. 'There are no roads in that area. You have to go on foot. A hundred years ago this whole area was the hunting ground of Shaka, the Zulu king, now it's a sanctuary for game, which includes white rhino that at one time nearly disappeared but now breed in such large numbers that they have to find homes for them elsewhere, all over the world. And lions that disappeared from this area entirely have begun to breed here again.'

'Lions?' said Edgar, delighted. 'Shall we see any, do you think?'

'With luck,' Ross replied, smiling. 'We shall go by car on the roads, of course. A wilderness trail unfortunately would take us too long. We'll go later in the afternoon when the heat of the day is over.'

Ross turned to Taryn and spoke softly to her.

'You're quiet, Taryn. Is this as good as the city?'

He was looking at her with that intense gaze of his black-fringed dark blue eyes.

'Much, much better,' she said.

When the sun had lost its sting, later in the afternoon, they set out in the minibus to traverse the roads, looking for animals. They did not have to wait long. Quite near the camp was a group of waterbuck, the males with curving horns of perfect symmetry. As they turned to trot away, a distinctive round white marking could be seen on the rump. Further on they came across nyala.

'Those are females,' said Ross. 'You see the does are reddish colour with white stripy markings, but the males are completely different. They don't even look as if they belong to the same species. We shall probably see one soon.'

And sure enough they came across two, dark and shaggy with a white ridge on the back and creamy stripes. As they walked they tossed their horns before striding with stiltlike legs into the bush. Ross drove up another road, and the landscape changed, becoming more open. Suddenly quite close to their vehicle, they saw rhinos. Ross had told them they could expect to see them, but no anticipation could reveal the astonishment they all felt when they were actually there in front of them.

'They can't be true,' said Melinda, giggling a little from fright.

'These are the square-lipped rhinos, quite harmless unless aroused in anger,' Ross told them, smiling at everyone's surprise.

'I must get a good shot of them,' said Brad. 'Just wait until I show them this back home!'

Edgar's ciné whirred too. There was something prehistoric and completely unreal about the huge creatures with their fantastic bulk and small eyes set in a head that bore one immense curved horn and one smaller straight one above the truculent square jaw. All at once they were disturbed by the sound of the whirring cameras and quickly formed themselves into a defensive circle, then trotted away, their large bulk heaving from side to side.

'Now where are those lions?' Edgar demanded, but in spite of the fact that they saw pug marks in the road and a place where a lion had been eating, only a vulture with a scraggy neck was left there picking at the white bones.

It was nearly evening when they came to a hide, a drinking hole, surrounded by trees. A long passage fenced with dense grass led to a wooden building on one side of the pool.

There were seats and narrow slits where those seated could get a good view of the water and the banks, without themselves being seen. Taryn found that, after the long trail up the grass passage, she was seated next to Ross with Melinda on his other side. She looked around for Coral and saw that she was sitting on the other side of the hut alone with Brad, who had his arm around her while he pointed out a nyala bull approaching the water. Well, Ross had said he wanted them to be charming to his guests, and Coral certainly seemed to be working at it.

But now Ross touched her hand and she became absorbed in the scene in front of her. Wet-nosed impala moved through the grass towards the water that was dappled with light and shade. Zebra came out into the open, but although they drank, they were obviously uneasy, tensed all the time for instant flight. High above on an old dead tree, a black and white fish eagle gave its haunting cry, then plummeted down to catch its prey, scattering a little group of warthogs who were cavorting around the edge.

They had to sit in absolute silence, and Taryn was very conscious of the man at her side, the touch of his hand as he gently motioned to her to look the other way at an approaching kudu, the warm breath on her face as she turned towards him. At last reluctantly they got up to go. They had to be back at the camp by sunset, for no tourists were allowed to be out after dark. As they drove in at the gate, Ross asked Taryn if she would go to the office to get another guide book for Trevor. He had already supplied one to Brad, and Trevor was keen to have one to identify all the animals he had shot on his ciné.

A Parks truck was parked in front of the office and, when Taryn went in, a familiar voice gave a delighted exclamation.

'Taryn, I was hoping I should see you. I heard that Ross had brought a party of visitors here, but I didn't know for certain that you'd come.'

It was Mike, his craggy face smiling down at her, his red hair ruffled as usual. Taryn was surprised how pleased she felt at seeing him.

'Mike, what on earth are you doing here? You're a long way from home.'

'I'm on leave for a few weeks. I know this seems an odd way to spend it coming from one reserve to another, but I have a friend here who's doing an investigation on lions, and I came to see how he's getting on. Later I hope to come to Durban. I was going to contact you there.'

'Are there lots of lions here, Mike? We haven't seen one yet.'

'Too many, it seems. Everyone was thrilled and delighted when they first arrived from the north and started breeding here, but now they're posing a bit of a problem, getting out and raiding for cattle on neighbouring farms and African lands. Phil, this friend of mine, is engaged in investigating how much space is needed for a certain number, and how much distance they cover. It's similar in a way to my study of eland. He darts them with a drug and tags them so they can be identified. As a matter of fact, we're going out to tag lions tonight. Would you like to come with us?'

Taryn was rather taken aback. 'Could I really come? It sounds exciting. But isn't it dangerous?'

'Not at all. You'll just sit on this truck. We won't expect you to get out and help us tag them. Phil has been doing it for ages and is expert at it. They don't approach the lions until they're absolutely out for the count. We take a vet with us as well.'

'All right, I'd simply love to come. But what about the others?'

'I can't really ask them. There are too many. Can't you slip out when they've gone to sleep? We only intend to go at about midnight, and you'll be back by three.'

The temptation to go with Mike was too hard to resist. Taryn felt she would never get such a chance again, to be out in the African night with men who knew the bush, and to see lions at close quarters. It would be something to remember all her life.

'Don't say anything to the others,' Mike warned. 'I'll meet you near the office. Even if they're aware that you've gone out, they'll just think you're going to the ablution block, won't they?'

'Mike is here,' Taryn told Ross when she took the guide to him.

'You look very pleased about it,' he commented dryly. 'Is that why you took so long? Amos here wants instructions on what to cook for dinner. What is it to be?'

'We brought fillet steak, and I suppose he can do chipped potatoes and a green salad with tomatoes. Will that do?'

'Admirably. So I shall open a bottle of red wine. Melinda and Coral have gone off to shower and I suppose that's what you want to do too, but don't take too long. We shall sit outside and see the moon rise.'

Coral monopolized the small mirror above the washbasin applying a make-up that seemed far too elaborate for the occasion. She had changed into a tight cotton knit black sweater worn with bright red slacks and a pearl choker, and she wound her hair in a complicated knot on top of her head. The total effect, Taryn had to admit, was beautiful. She and Melinda merely changed into their ordinary long-sleeved sweaters. They had to wait for Coral to finish at the mirror before they could comb their hair. Fortunately when she had finished, she went out and they saw her meet Brad and stand at the edge of the bush looking down over the wide valley. He put his arm around her and she laughed up at him.

'Why do men like women like Coral?' asked Melinda.

'Simply because she's beautiful, I suppose,' Taryn shrugged.

Melinda ran her brush through her shining golden hair.

'I intend to be beautiful too,' she said. 'But I won't be like Coral. All the same, it must be gorgeous to have men at your feet, mustn't it, Taryn?'

'A bit inconvenient, I should say,' Taryn replied, laughing.

At last she had her turn at the mirror. Yes, no woman could help envying another when she knew that the reflection from the mirror showed perfect features and shining beautiful hair. She looked with disfavour at her ordinary face with the wide brown eyes that Ross had likened to a giraffe's and the soft flyway brown hair that was nothing except mousy. It was certainly not her great beauty that had attracted Mike, she thought. She hoped she could get out tonight without arousing attention. It was good of Mike to ask her.

Just as Coral outshone the others in her dress, she excelled when it came to entertaining the guests. She sparkled, telling them stories of her visits to the States with a fashion show, and giving a very sophisticated impression. Ross sat back, leaving the conversation for the most part to Brad and Edgar and Coral. Taryn glanced at him every now and again wondering whether he minded that Brad was so obviously attracted to Coral. She would have thought a man of his temperament would be jealous. But then she supposed that he was very certain of Coral and that she was fulfilling the purpose for which he had brought her here by charming one of his guests.

The lights went off at ten from the main, but still they sat on at the table with the candles' glow enhancing Coral's beauty, gleaming on the gold of Mclinda's hair, giving a ruddy glow to Brad's handsome sunburned face, and throwing the shadow of Ross's eagle profile upon the wall but hiding the expression of those dark blue eyes. At last, to Taryn's relief, they made a move to go to bed. Just as well it is late, she thought, for she could keep awake without difficulty now. The others slept almost immediately. She could hear their light breathing. After a little while, the low laughter and chaffing from the men's hut died down. All was quiet. She could hear a nightjar calling its melancholy song a long way off – 'Good Lord deliver us,' Mike had once told her it said.

She got up quietly and took her slacks and top to the ablution block, where she changed. Then walking on the grass she made her way to the office. Mike stepped out of the shadows.

'Glad you were able to get away,' he said, taking her arm. 'They seemed to be staying up so late, I didn't think you'd make it. I'm afraid we'll have to walk down to the garage. We can't disturb the camp by starting up a truck engine at this time.'

He produced a torch and they walked some way down the road to the shed that was used for the trucks. There she was introduced to Phil and the vet. She and Mike climbed up into the back of the truck, where for company they had the bodies of two dead impala.

'Sorry about this,' said Mike as he saw her involuntary shudder. 'We have to have bait to attract the lions.'

They had chosen a place quite close to the hide where they had been during the afternoon as a likely place to find the lions.

'But we didn't see any signs of them this afternoon,' said Taryn.

'They were probably looking at you from the bush,' said Phil. 'There've been a large number around here lately.'

The dead carcasses were dragged along the road to make a scent trail, then left a few yards from the truck. After that they made the darting guns ready, charging them with the phials of drug that was used to make the animal unconscious. All lights were switched off and they sat in absolute darkness.

'Don't be scared at the noise you hear next,' Mike warned her.

A tape recorder had been attached to a tree and, when all was ready, it was switched on. Then followed the most terrifying sound of animals at a kill.

'But – but they aren't here already, are they?' asked Taryn.

'No, this is a tape. It attracts the lions to the meat, or so we hope.'

It was the most weird and ear-splitting din, and included the terrible noise of hyenas, screeches, screams, cackles, for all the world like a coven of witches on Walpurgis Night, and in addition there was the deep vibrating grunt of lions, quarrelling over their kill. When Taryn was feeling that she really could not stand it for another moment, the recorder was switched off.

'But . . . but . . .' she said, bewildered. 'There's still . . . oh!'

For Mike had switched on the headlights of the truck and

some other powerful lights too, and in the sudden glare they could see three lions pulling at the impala carcase. They did not seem in the least perturbed by the light but went on eating, trying to get as much for themselves as possible.

'Now comes the tricky part,' said Phil. He had his gun ready and the dart flew over the space, landing in a big male lion's rump. It gave an angry snarl and leapt away, disappearing into the darkness. 'He'll come back,' said Mike, and in a few moments he was back again, feeding on the meat as if nothing had happened.

'It can't hurt much,' said Taryn.

'It doesn't,' the vet assured her. 'We're able to calculate exactly how much is needed to put them to sleep. Watch what happens now.'

The lion was eating less avidly. Its great eyes, green and gold in the light of the truck, began to blink drowsily. Suddenly it keeled over and lay prostrate. Meanwhile Phil had darted the other animals and presently they were all comatose.

'It's safe now,' said the vet.

He and Phil got out of the truck and approached cautiously. There was no movement. Phil beckoned to Mike to come too, but Taryn was left in the truck while they took the measurements and fixed blue tags in the lions' ears.

'Now we shall have to wait for a while until they come round,' said Mike when he came back to Taryn.

'How about a little music?' suggested Phil.

He replaced the animal noises by a tape of classical music. To Taryn the whole experience had been fantastic. Here she was, in the middle of the African bush, surrounded by recumbent lions. All around the darkness was sinister with weird noises, the yelping cry of a jackal, the terrified shout of a baboon, and yet they sat listening to the heavenly sound of a symphony.

Presently the lions began to stir and then continued with their feast until there was nothing left but the gnawed bones. After this they slunk away into the darkness and the watchers were free to return to the camp. As Mike had said it would be, by this time it was three o'clock. Phil dropped them at the gate and Mike came in with Taryn.

'There's really no need to come with me,' she protested. 'I can find my way to the hut. I have a torch.'

'I'd prefer to see you safely back,' said Mike.

When they came within sight of the hut, Taryn said, 'It was wonderful. I can't thank you enough for taking me.'

'Not a word to the others, remember. This process is a bit hush-hush so far. Can I phone you when I come to Durban? Perhaps we can go out to dinner.'

'Of course,' she smiled.

While they had been walking across the uneven ground, he had put his arm around her and now he turned her to him and gave her a light kiss.

'Don't forget, it's a date,' he said.

She waved as he turned and set off on his way back to his part of the camp. And then she stood breathing in the cool night air, reluctant to go in after the excitement of the expedition. A voice spoke from the shadows.

'Mike seems to be more popular with you than I'd imagined, Taryn. I thought you said he didn't mean anything to you.'

'Oh, Ross, what a fright you gave me!'

'And you've given me a fright too. When Coral came to tell me you'd left the hut and that she'd found your night clothes in the ablution block, I simply couldn't think what you were up to. Then, of course, I remembered that Mike was here, so I gathered that you'd gone to keep a date with him.'

So Coral had spied on her. What was she to say?

'I was with Mike,' she admitted. 'He asked me if he could meet me this evening.'

'And I suppose because we sat late over dinner, we interfered with your plans. I'm astonished, Taryn, that you should think it conventional behaviour to meet a young man at this hour of the night.'

'I suppose it doesn't look too good, but, Ross, I can assure you there was no harm in it.'

He laughed scornfully. In the faint light his eyes glittered and his mouth had a bitter twist.

'Oh, for God's sake, Taryn, be your age! You've some-times seemed irresponsible since you came here, but until now I thought I could trust you. But I need convincing that a meeting with a man who's shown great interest in you can be classed as innocent at three o'clock in the morning.'

'You'll have to take my word for it. And let me tell you something, Ross. I'm not Melinda. You're not the guardian of my morals or my person. What I do in my free time is my own affair.'

'You think so? I need a woman of good character to look after Melinda.'

'I *am* of good character,' snapped Taryn. 'And whatever you may choose to think of me, Ross, you needn't let it worry you for very much longer. My time with you is nearly up and then I hope I can lead my own life without your interference.'

'You certainly can, and welcome to it,' said Ross, angrily.

'Do you want me to leave you?' asked Taryn.

It was fortunate that this scene was taking place in dark-ness, for she felt the tears start to her eyes.

'No, of course not. It would be too upsetting for Melinda at this time. I beg you to be more discreet. Do you intend to marry Mike?'

'That, Ross, is my affair,' said Taryn. 'And now I must get to bed. I'm dropping with weariness.'

She turned and went to the hut, letting herself in quietly. But, in spite of her words to Ross, she lay awake until the yellow light crept over the distant wilderness, not daring to weep in case she disturbed the other occupants.

143

CHAPTER TEN

As far as the two Americans were concerned, the week-end at the game reserve had been an unqualified success. The morning they left they saw three lions sleeping in the sun on a sand-spit further up the river from the bridge but still visible through the glasses.

'By gosh, they look tame,' Edgar exclaimed. 'They're so still I can't even use my ciné. I thought we'd get a bit more action from lions. Still, it's great to see them. Don't you want the glasses, Taryn?'

Taryn looked through the binoculars. She was still light-headed through lack of sleep. The three lions, stretched upon their sandbank, were oblivious of onlookers, lost in a deep doze like giant cats. As one flicked an ear to chase the flies she noticed a flash of blue.

'Fortunate beasts,' she murmured.

'You look tired, Taryn,' Coral commented maliciously. 'Didn't you get enough rest last night?'

'I guess we can't all look daisy-fresh like one person I could name,' said Brad.

Coral had clearly attracted him very much. Perhaps, thought Taryn, that accounted for the fact that Ross was quiet and seemed to be suffering from a depressed mood that he tried to shake off in conversation with his guests.

A few days later he came to the apartment during the morning when Melinda was at school.

'Leave your chores, Taryn, I'm going to take you out to lunch. It's the only free time I have and I must talk to you.'

What now? thought Taryn.

'I can't go anywhere where you have to be well dressed,' she said hesitantly.

Ross frowned. 'Aren't you interested in dressing well? Isn't the salary I pay you adequate?'

'Oh, yes,' Taryn answered, feeling embarrassed. 'You see,

I won't be working for you for very much longer and I feel I must save in case I can't find a job immediately.'

'You don't think I'd let you starve, do you? Anyhow, put on those smart slacks you wore at the reserve and we'll go somewhere informal.'

Taryn rushed off to change. She knew he hated to be kept waiting, but she found time to apply a little make-up and brush her hair. When she looked at herself in the mirror, she saw that her eyes were shining and her cheeks glowing with a peachy radiance.

'There, you look lovely, in spite of your protests about having nothing to wear,' said Ross when he saw her. 'But isn't that the classic thing that women say?'

'In my case it's almost true,' Taryn confessed.

They drove along the coast north of Durban and her spirits lifted to happiness as she sat back on the seat that was fitted with white lambswool for coolness. The smooth engine purred along the wide highway and, to the right, deep blue waves curled into the sandy bays.

'These holiday resorts used to be small villages,' said Ross, pointing to the towering white blocks of hotels and apartments. They passed these, however, and came to a smaller settlement where there was an eating place right near the beach.

'I always think this place is rather intriguing,' said Ross. 'The items on the menu have their origin in Mauritius, they're something like French provincial cooking but have that touch of Creole influence.'

They sat at a table with red checked tablecloth, and studied the handwritten menu. After a vivacious friendly woman dressed in bright peasant skirt, black blouse and red kerchief, had welcomed them, she explained the menu in greater detail.

'The trouble here is that you never know what to leave out,' said Ross. 'But you can't do better than to start with bouillabaisse.'

This was a fish soup served in red enamel bowls and was followed by octopus cooked in a creamy wine sauce and served in scallop shells, then came cassoulet, a spicy mixture of beans, sausages, and all kinds of savoury things, served from a red casserole on to red enamel plates.

'It's a good thing you have a healthy appetite,' said Ross. 'I've never dared to bring Coral here.'

So here was one place that he had not been to with Coral. Taryn was surprised how pleased she was to hear this. But why had he asked her to come? Whatever he had to tell her, he was leaving it until after they had finished eating. It was when they were drinking strong black coffee from red mugs that he came to the point.

'I've had news,' he said, 'that I'm needed in New York and I may have to stay over there for quite a while. This has altered my plans a bit as regards the children. I've decided they should go to school now instead of waiting another couple of months as I'd intended. I'm sure they'll be all right. They seem to have got on well and have become accustomed to the new syllabus more quickly than I thought they would.'

Now that the blow had fallen, Taryn realized that she had always hoped that something would happen to prolong her stay with Ross and the family. It was foolish really to feel so much despair, for she had always known she would have to leave, but now that it was a reality, she felt so much sadness that she could not understand it herself. Was it only because he was going to New York that he was sending Melinda to school early, she wondered, or was there some other reason? Did he not trust her, Taryn, after she had been out late at night with Mike? In spite of her denials, she felt that he had been far from satisfied and thought she had behaved badly.

'When do you want me to leave?' she stammered.

'There's no hurry. I hope you'll stay to help Melinda buy her school uniforms. But of course once she's gone there'll be no need for you to stay on in the apartment. If you would like to work here in Durban, I could give you some introductions, but I think you would be happier if you returned to England.'

'How do you know what would make me happy?' asked Taryn bitterly.

He looked at her gravely, his blue eyes considering her, she thought, as if she were an insect in the game reserve that was of some interest to him.

'If you have a leaning towards Mike, of course I can see that you might want to stay here. It's for you to say.'

'I don't know that your letters of introduction would get me far,' she said, ignoring his last remark. 'I have no qualifications, as I've told you before, and there are few domestic jobs here.'

'Yes, I agree, I think on the whole it might be best if you were to return. But as I said, I don't know how you feel about Mike. You must realize that it's quite a hard life for a girl who's not used to this country to go and live in the wilds.'

'I don't think I'd mind it,' said Taryn.

She thought of the wide range of blue mountains that the Zulus had called the Wall of Spears and she thought of the clear pure air and the calls of birds high, wild and free, and as she did so her eyes took on a soft, dreamy look.

'I can see by your expression that you have some tender feeling for Mike,' said Ross. 'So if that's what you want you must go for it. All the same, I have a proposition to make to you. I shall leave instructions at the office that if you need an air ticket to England you must have it. Otherwise if I come back from New York and find you engaged to Mike, you shall have the amount of the fare for a wedding present.'

'It's good of you, but you don't owe me anything,' Taryn denied.

'That's for me to decide.' Ross put his hand across the table and took hers in a strong, warm grasp. 'You've given me quite a lot of pleasure as well as pain. I haven't known a girl who could appreciate new sights and sounds and scenery as much as you, Taryn. I've enjoyed seeing those huge brown eyes sparkle with delight, even if it's at such a simple thing as the meal we've just had.'

'And the pain?' asked Taryn.

'We'll pass over that, I think. Don't let's rake up old differences. It's too late now.'

Yes, it was far too late, thought Taryn, too late to realize in a blinding flash that this man, sitting so quietly grasping her hand and smiling into her eyes, meant far too much to her, more than life itself. How could she have been so blind? Only now when she was going to have to leave him for ever did she know that from the first moment she had seen him he had held for her this perilous attraction. But it had always been too late. She had never had a chance. He could never love her. He did not even like her much. She had always seemed to be at cross purposes with him, always in the wrong.

Why then did he have this terrible power to attract her? She could not understand it. It was beyond explanation. Now she knew why she had always felt so happy in his presence, why she had missed him so much when he was away. And now he was to be away from her for the rest of her life. She would have to go through it knowing that somewhere on the other side of the world, he was there, smiling into Coral's emerald eyes as he was looking at her now, but with such a different expression.

How could she have fallen in love with a man who so obviously belonged to someone else? It was a good thing she was going, and yet she could not bear the thought of it. She would have to get used to living in the ordinary humdrum world away from this constant enchantment, this existence made exciting by the fact that there was always a chance of seeing Ross and of finding delight in his company.

'What are you thinking of so deeply?' Ross asked, still grasping her hand. 'There's no need to worry, Taryn. I'm sure you'll get along fine, but don't forget, any time you want your ticket to England, it's there for the asking.'

As they drove home, he said, 'You're very quiet. I'm going to arrange a party which will serve to entertain our American friends but also be in the nature of a farewell for you and for Melinda before she goes to school. There's a charity affair at one of the hotels next week. Coral is to model in the fashion show. I think it will be a suitable occasion for Melinda, better than an ordinary visit to a night club, which is not very appropriate for a young girl.'

Taryn wondered what she could wear. Obviously it would

be an affair that required evening dress, and what would be the use of spending part of her savings on an outfit that she would probably never require again?

It was as if Ross read her thoughts, for he added, 'You and Melinda must go to a dress shop and buy new evening gowns and the accessories to go with them. It's in the nature of a business occasion too. I'm entertaining a party of American associates, including our friends, and I want you and Melinda to be well dressed. In fact I think I shall come with you when you go to buy the dresses. Otherwise we'll probably find that Melinda spends too much and you spend too little.'

'Are you going to tell Melinda about the new arrangements or shall I?' asked Taryn, when they reached the apartment.

'I'll leave it to you. Now I must go. I'm already late for an important appointment. Good-bye, Taryn, it was a good lunch, wasn't it?'

She walked slowly to the lift, not looking back although she had not heard the car start. Melinda had come back and left a note. 'I'm going out. May be a bit late.'

It was careless of her not to say where she was going, but Taryn felt glad to be alone for a while. She prepared supper in the late afternoon, and while she was waiting for Melinda, she did something that was most unusual for her, and poured herself a glass of sherry. She went to sit on the patio, sipping it slowly and watching the first faint stars appear above the rooftops. She must think over in solitude the emotions she had experienced this afternoon.

She thought of Ross saying, 'It was a good lunch, wasn't it?' Yes, that was all it had meant to him. He had taken her out there wanting to soften the blow, wanting to put her into a good mood before he delivered his ultimatum. But she was being foolish. She had known all along that this could not last much longer. So why then should she feel as if she were being cast into the desert? This sudden overwhelming passion she had felt ... surely could not be love? She had never felt before anything approaching it.

For Mike she had felt a kindly affection. She had even

thought she might be happy with him, a peaceful, even kind of contentment. But that had nothing to do with the wild feeling that had rushed into her heart when she had been told that she was to part from Ross for ever. Suddenly she had realized that he was inexpressibly dear to her. And what was she to do about it? Nothing. She must get over it as one got over an illness. She must get away as soon as possible and never see him again, and some day, somewhere, she would climb out of this dark valley of despair that she felt all around her.

Darkness had come while she was engrossed in these bitter thoughts, and with a start she realized that Melinda was much later than usual. Now she began to worry for a different reason. She had never before been so late. The dinner was drying in the warming oven and still she waited. At last she remembered the name of one of Melinda's friends and phoned the number.

'Melinda? No, I haven't seen her today at all,' Vanessa said when she was called to the phone.

'But surely you saw her in class?'

'Oh, yes, of course,' said the girl quickly.

There was something about the tone of her voice that made Taryn puzzled.

'She's been to the beach every day this week,' said Taryn. 'I thought she usually went with you.'

'Oh, yes, she does. But I think this week she was with another friend – I've forgotten her name.'

'Please try to remember it,' said Taryn. 'It's dark and late and I'm rather worried about her.'

'I'm sure she'll be back soon. She must have forgotten the time,' said Vanessa. It was obvious to Taryn that the girl knew something that she didn't want to say.

'Perhaps you'll try to remember the name of the other girl with whom Melinda is friendly and give me a ring,' Taryn suggested.

'Yes, I'll do that,' said Vanessa, and quickly put down the phone.

A few minutes later Melinda came in. She looked lovely, her gold hair tangled, her blue eyes sparkling and her face radiant.

'Sorry I'm late,' she said. 'I had some supper at Vanessa's.'

'I've just been speaking to Vanessa and she said she hadn't seen you today,' said Taryn sternly.

'How silly of me! I said Vanessa, but I meant Veronica. I get mixed up with having two friends whose names start with a V.'

'Melinda, are you being truthful with me?'

'Why shouldn't I be?' asked Melinda. She looked like an untidy angel, her eyes blue, wide and innocent. 'Why are you fussing, Taryn? I've only been down to the beach with friends and we all had a hamburger at the coffee bar. I thought you wouldn't like it if I said I'd been to a place like that for supper, so I told you I'd been to Vanessa's.'

'I wish you wouldn't make up stories to suit yourself, Melinda. I would much rather know what you're doing.'

'I'd tell you if you and Ross didn't fuss so much,' complained Melinda. 'You make me want to break out, between you. Sometimes I think I'll be freer when I go to this boarding school.'

'Ross called and took me out to lunch,' said Taryn.

'Lucky you! I wish I'd been here.'

'He says he has arranged that you should go to this school the week after next, sooner than he'd intended.'

Melinda's face was suddenly still with shock.

'No, he can't mean it! I thought I was to stay here for ages yet.'

'That's what he's decided.'

'Oh, he is a tyrant, just as I'm getting used to it here! What about all my friends? It will be awful to make new ones over again. And what about the beach? I'll miss it terribly.'

'I thought you just said you'd feel freer if you went to boarding school. A few moments ago you were moaning about my fussing,' Taryn pointed out.

'I didn't mean it, Taryn, you know I didn't. We've been so happy here. Oh, why does everything have to change? Why can't it stay the same?'

Melinda burst into a sudden storm of tears and rushed to

her room, where she refused all Taryn's attempts at comforting her.

Nothing can ever stay the same, thought Taryn. And we never realize how happy we've been until it's over. At Silver Ridge she had often felt worried and doubtful, but now when she thought of her life at the house in its encircling blue hills, where every day she had met and spoken to Ross, it seemed like a heavenly dream.

Melinda did not seem as thrilled as Taryn had thought she would be at the thought of going to the charity dinner with Ross and the Americans.

'I thought you were always pressing Ross to take you to one of the big hotels to some function,' said Taryn.

'I've grown out of that. I guess I was childish then. Now I like to be with people of my own age. Besides, I'm not all that keen on seeing Coral charming all the men. She makes me feel ill.'

'She won't be with us all the time. She's to be in the fashion parade.'

'And all the men will be telling her how marvellous she looked in the dresses, I know. You can't win with Coral.'

But Melinda brightened up when Ross arrived to take them shopping for their dresses. They went to a small boutique, and Taryn felt quite horrified when she saw the discreetly displayed prices.

'I could buy a secondhand car for this!' she exclaimed.

Ross laughed heartily.

'Don't think about it. Just try on the dresses. I'm here to write the cheque.'

'White for Melinda,' Ross suggested. 'We must show up that tan.'

They found a cool plain white crêpe dress for her. It had a halter neck that showed her lovely young brown back.

'I hope they allow it at the school dance,' said Melinda. 'It's gorgeous. Thanks, Ross. You aren't such an ogre in spite of everything.'

She twined her arms around his neck and kissed him.

'Well,' grinned Ross, 'if I get such a reward I'd better come to buy dresses more often. How about it, Taryn?'

She had come out to show him the dress that the sales-woman had told her was the most becoming. She walked shyly towards him, not meeting his eyes. It was a lovely dress with a high-cut bodice that made it look like something in a mediaeval painting. It was of a very dark brown, almost black, gauzy material with a small design in gold, cut with a scooped neckline that showed her young brown throat, and with sleeves that reached to the elbows. It made Taryn feel excitingly different.

'Yes, indeed, Taryn, that's the dress,' said Ross.

Now she lifted her head and met his eyes, that were a little surprised and held an admiring expression. She could not remember that he had ever looked at her in this way before.

'Are you pleased with it yourself? Do you really like it?' he asked.

'Of course, who wouldn't?' she said.

'So how about my reward?' he asked, smiling wickedly. 'Melinda gave me a hug and a kiss.'

'Perhaps later,' she found the courage to say.

'I shall hold you to it.'

The saleslady came bustling up with gold shoes and handbag and silver ones for Melinda.

'I always tell my customers to ask themselves three questions,' she said. 'Does it fit me? Does it suit me? and then the most vital of all, Do I really love it? I think I can say your dresses answer all the questions, don't you?'

The next week sped quickly, too quickly, past. Taryn decided that when Melinda had left for school, she would stay at some small place while she was seeking work and, with this in mind, she booked a room a short bus ride from the town. But she did not tell anyone she had done this. She was afraid Ross would say she could stay for a while, and she did not want this. She must make the break in a determined way, and the best time was when Melinda left. Otherwise she might be tempted to linger and would become a nuisance to Ross.

On the day of the party, Taryn made an appointment with a hairdresser. He held the strands of her soft honey brown hair and clucked deprecatingly over it.

'Lovely texture, but it's had far too much sun and is wickedly neglected. I'll have to thin it a bit if you want it styled.'

Taryn sat feeling rather scared while he snipped away and a great quantity of hair fell upon the floor.

'I hope I shall have some left,' she said anxiously.

'Plenty. You'll be surprised.'

And she was. He styled it into a lovely swirl that showed up the beautiful shape of her small head and somehow emphasized her large luminous eyes. Next she went to a make-up counter where she purchased a soft apricot make-up that flattered her gentle colouring.

The result was amazing, she thought, as she sat in front of the mirror putting the finishing touches to her dressing. It was seven-fifteen and Ross was to call for them at seven-thirty. She was surprised therefore when she saw in the mirror that Melinda had strolled into her room and was still in her blue jeans she had worn all day. She looked flushed and embarrassed.

'Melinda, whatever is the matter? Why haven't you changed yet?'

'I don't feel well, Taryn. I think it was the toasted sandwich I had at lunchtime. I feel a bit sick and I have a headache. I'll be fine if I stay home but I just can't face going to the hotel.'

'Oh, Melinda, what bad luck! Are you sure you won't feel better if I give you an aspirin?'

'I've had two already. I'm sorry, Taryn, I just can't go.'

'But I can't leave you here by yourself feeling ill.'

'Of course you can. I shall be quite all right. You can't let Ross down. One person is bad enough. It will ruin his party if you don't go. You look quite wonderful, Taryn. I'm so glad. Coral is going to be green with envy when she sees you.'

'You look flushed, Melinda. Poor dear, do go and lie down.'

'I'll do that. Those aspirins have made me feel sleepy.'

'Can I get you some Bovril and dry toast?'

'No, Taryn, I just want to sleep. Please don't worry about me. I don't want to see Ross. Will you do the explaining? Tell him I shall phone the hotel if I need you.'

Ross was naturally very taken aback when Taryn broke the news to him that Melinda could not come.

'She says she's all right and she hasn't got a temperature, but she doesn't think she could face a dinner at the hotel. Do you think I should stay with her? She doesn't seem to want me to do that.'

'There's no need. She can easily phone us if she wants us. Or she can phone down to the porter and I'll tell him he must ask for us if she needs us. But from what you tell me, she'll be all right. She's probably been overdoing things. She's always flying down to the beach, isn't she? It may be a touch of the sun. If she's no better in the morning, we'll get a doctor.'

Taryn still felt uneasy, but Ross insisted that she should go, and Melinda, lying in her bed and not looking very ill, supported him.

'Is Ross mad at me?' she asked Taryn.

'Of course not, but of course he's disappointed. He'd planned this as a treat before you go to school.'

'But it wasn't just for me,' Melinda insisted. 'He needed to entertain these Americans and he'd promised Coral he would support this charity show. And of course it will be your last outing with him too. Oh, Taryn, aren't you sorry to leave us all?'

'Of course I am. Now settle down and try to sleep. And if you need us don't hesitate to phone the hall porter. He'll get a message through to us.'

Taryn went back to Ross in the living-room.

'Well now, let me look at you.'

His eyes were upon her, examining her from top to toe, it seemed, in a long, long look. For once she felt confident and charming. How wonderful life would be if you could always feel like this, she thought.

'Will I do?' she asked.

He took her hands and again looked at her as if he had never seen her before.

'Isn't she beautiful?' he asked the empty room. 'Isn't she lovely?'

Taryn closed her eyes before the admiration she saw in his.

'It's the dress,' she said. 'Anyone would look wonderful in it.'

'Not anyone. Just you, Taryn. It was made for someone like you with your soft colouring and your gentle expression. And what did they do to that fly-away hair of yours?'

She lifted her hand to her hair in embarrassment.

'No, don't touch it. I can see that, simple as the style is, it's a work of art. For the first time since I've known you, Taryn, you look like a woman, and an alluring one at that.'

She walked away from him and started turning out the lights that were unnecessary if they were going out. She left two small lamps burning and the rest of the room was in shadow when she turned and said, 'There, I think we can go now.'

'Did you hear what I said?'

Ross was standing near her, but she could not interpret his expression, she was only very aware of his eyes, almost black in this light, and the smiling curve of his mouth.

'Yes, I heard,' she replied. 'I'm glad I don't look young any more, because certainly I don't feel young.'

'I said you looked alluring, Taryn. It has nothing to do with looking old or young.'

'That's very kind of you, Ross. But it's all due to the dress you bought for me – you must realize that. Tomorrow I shall be the same Taryn who's irresponsible and looks too young and always manages to do things wrong.'

'I don't care about tomorrow,' said Ross. 'The important time is now.'

And then he was kissing her, a kiss that lasted, it seemed to Taryn, a long, long time and yet was over in a few moments. How had it come to this? She did not know. She only knew that here was something else that would be imprinted on her mind, another bitter-sweet memory she was to carry like a scar for her whole life long.

'Taryn,' he whispered, 'sweet, sweet Taryn. But it was you who owed me a kiss, remember, a kiss for the dress. Now when am I to get it?'

'Not now,' said Taryn. 'The others will be waiting.'

Of course, he had only been teasing her again. She should have known it. It had been just a kiss to him, a kiss he had given her because tonight she looked charming. Beautiful, he had said. How could I look beautiful? she wondered. And yet for a while, for those few short moments, when he held me in his arms, I felt the most beautiful woman in the world.

CHAPTER ELEVEN

SHE leaned back against the cream lambswool of her seat and closed her eyes as Ross drove swiftly and competently towards the hotel.

'Coral had to go early,' he told her. 'Of course as she's appearing in the fashion parade, she had to see that her clothes were arranged properly. Our guests are staying just a few steps away at another hotel along the beach front.'

Coral. Taryn had forgotten about her. She would be at the dinner tonight, flirting with Brad but at the same time showing everyone that it was really Ross who belonged to her. How could she endure it? But she must. The ordeal would soon be over.

The room where the function was to be held was a large ballroom glittering with crystal chandeliers and festooned with blue velvet curtains with great swags of gold braid looping them away from the windows, through which one could see the sparkling lights along the promenade and the dark expanse of ocean beyond. Along the length of the room was a raised dais for the fashion parade, and circular tables were set around this set with blue tablecloths and gilt tableware and candlesticks.

The whole effect was extremely luxurious and the crowd who were attending this charity function were very well dressed, many of the women wearing mink capes even though outside the weather was warm. Inside the ballroom, however, the air-conditioning chilled the atmosphere. Even amongst this bevy of elegant women, Coral was outstanding. As she swept across the room to join their party, many eyes followed her, in her startling dress of emerald green with its sleeves slashed to show a lining of silver.

She greeted the men enthusiastically but hardly acknowledged Taryn, until suddenly seeming to become aware of her presence, she said, 'Taryn, I've never seen you looking so well dressed before. Wait until your admirer sees you.

You must have known he would be here tonight.'

'My admirer?' queried Taryn.

'Mike, of course. Surely you must have known he was to be here? I saw him with a party of people in the bar down-stairs. It seems a strange place to meet an out-of-doors chap like him, but doubtless he had his reasons for coming.'

It did seem strange that Mike should be here, but he had mentioned that he was coming to Durban. They had no sooner been served with their aperitifs than he came to the table. He looked a little ill at ease in his black dinner jacket. Taryn thought he looked much better in ranger's uniform. He was introduced to the others, but had eyes only for Taryn.

'Taryn, you look wonderful! Coral said you were going to be here. I'm with my brother and his wife. It isn't exactly my thing, but I'm glad to see you. Can I claim a dance later?'

'Yes, of course, Mike.'

Ross was looking at them and did not seem too pleased that they were conversing together in low voices. Taryn supposed he might think she was neglecting his guests.

'I'll see you later, Mike,' she said aloud.

Besides Brad and Edgar, Ross had asked some other people who were visiting Durban for the first time. They were all very pleasant to Taryn, unlike Coral, who ignored her for the most part but every now and again managed to slip in some waspish remark.

'I'm surprised that Melinda didn't come,' she said. 'It's hard luck that she should be left alone if she's not feeling well. I'm sure Ross could have managed without you if you'd insisted on staying. But of course it was an oppor-tunity to meet Mike, wasn't it?'

'I didn't know Mike was coming,' Taryn told her.

'No? But I'm sure he must have known you were. It looks as if he had to borrow a dinner jacket for the occasion, doesn't it?'

'I expect he did,' Taryn replied tranquilly.

She was determined not to be riled by Coral. She would enjoy this evening, or at least she would try, for she had never in her life been to such a luxurious function before and never worn such a beautiful dress or felt that she looked . . . what was it Ross had said? . . . alluring.

The dinner that followed was magnificent. There was smoked salmon rolled with its filling of Beluga caviare and sour cream, fresh trout brought from the mountain streams, crayfish tails in cream sauce with mushrooms, rare tender sirloin, fillet stuffed with oysters. If Ross had wanted to impress his friends from America, this was certainly the occasion to do so. Coral had gone off to change into her clothes for the fashion show, and for the first time since they had arrived, Taryn found herself with Ross.

'Do you think I should phone Melinda before the show starts?' she asked.

Ross shook his head and squeezed her arm reassuringly. 'Not to worry. Melinda will phone if she needs us. You'll only disturb her if you phone now. She's probably asleep.'

He left her and went over to talk to some of his guests. Taryn looked after him. Why did he make such an impression on her? Why did she find it difficult to keep her eyes from him? She was so conscious of that tall slim broad-shouldered figure in the custom-made black suit, the white shirt showing up the dark brown of his face and the glossy dark chestnut hair that was so beautifully groomed. Why did he have so much appeal for her? Surely she was not a schoolgirl to be charmed by good looks? She must talk to the other guests. Almost feverishly she started chatting to Edgar, who was amiable and talkative and not in the least handsome.

The fashion show followed and of course Coral was the star. Whatever she wore she was magnificent, and the clothes were unusual and distinctive by a new young designer, silk kaftans with beautiful designs and jewel colours, flowing around the body with subtle defining cut, gorgeous furs, made from black Swakara lamb with deep edgings of pearl-coloured mink. Coral came back to their table in triumph, for all the clothes she had worn had been sold.

Meanwhile the ramp had been cleared and the room was set for dancing.

'You were wonderful,' Brad told Coral. 'Am I allowed the first dance? I must get a bit of reflected glory by claiming the star of the show.'

Coral laughed up at him. 'If Ross doesn't mind.'

'Don't take any notice of Ross. He must put his guests' pleasure first.'

They danced away, smiling into each other's eyes.

'Tough, Ross,' said Edgar. 'If you don't look out you'll be losing your girl-friend, Brad is really turned on about her.'

Ross smiled with a lazy, amused grin. I suppose he's so confident, thought Taryn, that he can afford to let Coral go off with Brad. It doesn't seem to worry him much, or perhaps he hides his feelings. As I do mine.

'Don't be so thoughtful, Taryn. Here's a young man dying to dance with you,' said Ross.

He handed her over to Edgar and then sat watching the dancers with an enigmatic smile. Edgar was light and deft with his feet. There was hardly time for any conversation while she followed the jazzy rhythm.

'You look lovely,' he shouted above the sound of the organ and the guitars. 'A bit different from the game reserve, this, isn't it?'

Mike danced past with a tall fair girl and Edgar hailed him like a long-lost friend, although he had barely met him at the game reserve.

'Can't get away from you chaps, can we? One moment you're acting the tough game warden, then the next we find you at a do like this.'

'Between ourselves, I prefer the wilds,' Mike answered. 'Taryn, this is my sister-in-law Margot. May I claim that dance next?'

Taryn nodded her head and was whirled away by Edgar. She glanced over to Ross. He was still sitting at the table talking to the other Americans and seemed to have stopped watching the dancers. When the dance ended, Brad and Coral disappeared in the direction of the long curving bar that was at one end of the room. Edgar restored Taryn to her seat and said, 'That was great. We must have another go later.'

The music started again and still Coral lingered at the other end of the room with Brad.

'Come along, Taryn. I know you dance well. We've tried before, haven't we?'

Ross stood in front of her, his smile inviting. His arms were open, waiting for her to come into them, but she could not go. She could not let Mike down, Mike, who was making his way across the crowded room with eyes only for her.

'I'm sorry, Ross, but Mike asked me to have this dance with him.'

His face was expressionless as Mike took her away. She felt regret out of all proportion to its cause. Why, oh, why had Mike asked her for this dance when she could have been dancing with Ross? She saw Ross asking one of the American girls to dance and in a few moments they were whirling around the floor, with Ross laughing into the eyes of his pretty partner.

'I don't dance very well, you may remember from that other time,' Mike apologized to her. 'But I had to dance with you tonight, Taryn. You're looking simply stunning. What a wonderful dress!'

'Ross bought it. I couldn't have afforded this from my salary.'

Mike frowned.

'Don't look like that. He said it was a business occasion and he wanted Melinda and me to look grand.'

'Well, he would hardly miss it, would he? Where's Melinda, by the way?'

'The poor child got ill. She wasn't able to come.'

'I saw her the other day. I don't know whether I'm telling tales out of school. She and a young boy were looking very affectionate together on the beach.'

'Melinda? I'm sure you must be mistaken. She says she hardly ever meets any boys.'

'Perhaps I am. There are quite a lot of young girls with long blonde hair in Durban. It's difficult to tell them apart.'

'Anyway, she's leaving Durban in a few days' time to go to boarding school.'

'And you?'

'I don't know, Mike. I haven't made up my mind what to do. I shall be leaving Ross, of course.'

She had decided not to tell anyone where she was going. She felt she wanted to get away from everyone she had known at Silver Ridge.

'Will you let me know what you've decided when the time comes?'

'Yes, I shall do that,' she replied, feeling guilty that she was telling him a lie. 'Ross is going to America for a while.'

'So you'll be on your own again.'

'I've always been on my own,' she said.

'You didn't fall for your employer's charm? But I know, Taryn, you have more sense than to do that.'

It was just as well that Mike had never realized how she felt about Ross. No one must realize it. She had only just discovered it herself. She smiled at Mike as he took her back to her table and left her there. Ross, standing by, must have heard his last words, 'I shall see you again, Taryn.'

But Ross was looking at Coral who was crossing the floor and came to him as if she had been seeking him for a long time.

'Oh, Ross darling, have you been missing me? Brad and I were having such a long interesting conversation. You mustn't mind. Now you shall have my whole attention for at least a quarter of an hour.'

She smiled teasingly up at him, looking quite enchanting, her emerald eyes brilliant. And they went off together, swaying gracefully, her slim white hands clasped behind his brown neck, his hands on her waist. Taryn was left alone. I've always been on my own, she had said to Mike. And that was true. But she dreaded to think of the future now, when she would have to leave her present position with all its sorrows and all its joys, for some humdrum work in the city.

The other guests were all dancing and somehow it had been overlooked that she had been left out. Not that she minded. She sat and gazed at the crowded ballroom, the kaleidoscope of colour as the elegant women in the pretty dresses swirled past. There was Ross, with eyes only for Coral. They looked such a perfectly matched pair. She could see other people were noticing them too.

As long as she was here in the ballroom, she could not keep her eyes off them, so she decided to walk to one of the french windows that led on to the balcony, and look down on the crowded scene of the beach front with all its glittering lights. No one else was there, for it seemed everyone was dancing. After the chill of the ballroom, the air was soft and warm outside and Taryn was quite alone. She leaned over the low wall and looked at the scene below her.

Although by now it was late, crowds of people were still walking along the sea-front enjoying the night air. She noticed there were many young people in couples, boys and girls dressed in almost identical blue jeans and vest tops, the boys with shoulder-length hair and sometimes beards, the girls with hair brushed straight and long half-way down their backs. It was quite true, as Mike had said, that all the girls looked rather alike, for there was one down there who looked very like Melinda from a distance with her long blonde hair and faded denim slacks.

The young girl in question was clinging affectionately to a tall blond boy dressed in the knee-length baggy trousers they used for surfing. The boy said something to her and the girl laughed, flinging back her head in a gesture that Taryn recognized. It was Melinda. But how could it be? They had left her safely at home in bed. Surely it could not be the same girl strolling along the sea-front with this boy holding her around the waist in an intimate fashion that spoke of a close relationship. As Taryn stood dumbstruck, they disappeared in the crowd. And in the next moment, as she was debating what was best to do, she was aware that Ross had come out and was standing at her side.

'So this is where you've disappeared to? Coral has ideas about going on to a nightclub. This party seems to be over now, but the night is still young.'

'I think I should go back to Melinda,' said Taryn.

Now that the pair had vanished below her, she could not

164

bring herself to believe that she was not mistaken. She must go back and find out. Should she tell Ross her suspicions? But no, he would just think she was imagining things, as perhaps she was.

'Nonsense,' said Ross. 'And it's no use phoning her to disturb her. She'll be fast asleep. We should have heard about it long ago if anything was wrong. Come along, we'll go to the nightclub first. I promise we won't stay long. But the party is going a bit dead on us here. It needs an injection of new life before we all separate.'

He had hold of her arm and reluctantly she turned to go back into the ballroom. As Ross had said, people seemed to be going home now, for the show was over, but the people in their party were still lively and ready for anything. The others said they would go back to their hotel to get extra cars, but Brad commandeered Coral while Ross went to get his car, saying he would see them at the front of the hotel. Taryn found herself in the foyer waiting with Coral and Brad. She still felt uneasy. Could it possibly be Melinda that she had seen? Brad and Coral were chatting, quite oblivious of her presence, when suddenly in the crowd she caught a glimpse of Mike, who was on his own. He seemed to be looking around. Perhaps he was looking for her? She darted through the crowd and caught hold of his arm.

'Mike!'

'Oh, Taryn. I was hoping to catch you before you left.'

'I'm so glad I met you. I feel worried about Melinda. The others are going on to a nightclub, but I feel uneasy because she wasn't well when I left home. Do you think you could possibly take me home? I don't want to break up Ross's party, but I should like to see if she's all right.'

Still she would not admit to herself or to him that she feared Melinda might not be there.

'Of course, Taryn. It would give me the greatest pleasure to take you. But what about Ross? Won't he object?'

'I shall tell Coral I'm going and she can explain to Ross. I'm sure he won't mind. He doesn't really need me.'

He never has needed me, she thought, and now even less. But she thrust these thoughts aside and got into Mike's car, glad to be heading for the apartment.

On the way there she decided she had better confide something of her fears to Mike.

'You'll think I'm crazy,' she said, 'but I thought I saw Melinda with a young man on the beach-front. I know it's stupid, but I feel uneasy. I won't be happy until I see she's safely in bed.'

They reached the apartment block and spoke to the sleepy guard who was on duty there.

'Miss Melinda must be well,' he said. 'You said to phone if she needed you, but I think she sleeps.'

The lift whirred up to the top floor and Mike took the key from Taryn. She rushed into the apartment, going straight to Melinda's bedroom, walking in quietly. There was no one there. She looked in the bathroom, but it was empty. Melinda's short nightdress was on the bed. She came back to Mike, her eyes wide and stricken.

'She's gone out. Oh, how could she? What am I to do?'

Mike put his arm around her and gave her a little shake.

'Taryn, don't look as if it's the end of the world. Melinda is just playing truant because you were at the party. I'm sure she intends to be back soon.'

'But Ross will be furious if he finds out. I must find her before he comes home. She must have some boy-friend that she's kept secret from me. He'll blame me for this.'

'What a tyrant he always seems to you! Now stop worrying. We'll go back to the beach and search carefully along there. They'll spend a couple of hours at the nightclub. If we get her back before that, he need never know.'

Back at the beach, they parked the car on the front and started walking. It was less crowded now and many of the young people had gone. People turned to look at Taryn in her beautiful dress with her distraught expression, but she was unaware of this.

'Where can we look now?' she asked.

'We'll try the discothèque,' Mike suggested.

But though they stood at the door and watched the dancers gyrating to the deafening music there was never a glimpse of Melinda.

'It's hopeless,' said Taryn finally. 'We shall have to give up and I shall have to face Ross and tell him Melinda is missing.'

Then, just as they were returning to the parked car, Taryn saw a figure in the distance hurrying towards them. It looked like Melinda and she was alone. Taryn started running as best she could, picking up her long dress and hurrying to make sure that it was really Melinda. When she saw Taryn she burst into tears.

'Oh, Taryn, is it really you? I didn't know how I was going to get home. Donald got annoyed with me because I wouldn't let him park at a lonely place near the beach. And he left me to get back alone. I seem to have been walking for hours!'

'You can tell Taryn about it tomorrow. The important thing now is to get back before Ross. Taryn says he's sleeping at the apartment tonight,' said Mike.

'Oh, yes, I must have been crazy, but Donald persuaded me to say I was ill and miss the party so I could meet him. I didn't realize he could be so awful. He said it was our last chance because I was going to school. Oh, Taryn, I've been such a fool!'

'Don't cry any more. Let's go home while we can,' said Taryn.

As they were turning into the road that led to the apartment block, Mike suddenly braked.

'What's wrong?' asked Taryn.

'Ross's car was just ahead of us. He's turning in to go to the garage now.'

'How did you get out without the guard seeing you?' Taryn asked Melinda.

'I came down the fire escape.'

'Then you'd better go up the same way. It's at the side of the building and Ross won't see you. Meanwhile I shall go up in the ordinary way and meet him in the apartment. You go straight into your room and don't turn the light on.'

'Do you want me to come up?' asked Mike.

'No, better not. I can't thank you enough, Mike, for what

you did tonight.'

She put her hands on his shoulders and gave him a kiss. He smiled, his craggy face kind, his blue eyes very affectionate.

'That was a nice surprise. It made my evening really worthwhile. I'll phone you tomorrow. Good-bye, my dear, dear Taryn.'

He put his arms around her and kissed her tenderly. Taryn turned to go inside and was suddenly aware that Ross was standing a few yards away. She had thought he would come in at the back, but he had come along the pavement and was waiting there because they were in the doorway blocking his entrance. He swung his car keys and came towards them.

'Good evening, Mike, won't you come up for a drink? Why is Taryn keeping you outside? I can assure you, you would have more privacy upstairs. Personally I intend to get to bed as soon as possible, so I can guarantee I shouldn't be in the way.'

'Thanks, Ross, but I must be off. Good-bye, Taryn. I'll give you a ring tomorrow.'

Ross had seemed quite affable with Mike and looked perfectly normal when he was speaking to him, but when they were in the lift he neither smiled nor spoke to Taryn and they entered the apartment in silence.

'I'll just go and see if Melinda is all right,' Taryn said, and hurried to the girl's room. Incredible as it seemed, Melinda was fast asleep in her bed, her clothes scattered over the floor, breathing lightly and peacefully and looking as if she did not have a care in the world. Taryn came back to the living room. Ross was standing at the window looking out over the wide view of the city and she had to speak before he noticed her.

'Can I get you anything to drink, Ross? Do you want some coffee?'

He turned round, and she was shocked by the coldness of his expression.

'Not now, Taryn. It's late and we've had a long evening. But why did you tell Coral you were coming home to Mel-

168

inda when you really intended to be alone with Mike?'

Taryn could not think of any explanation that would be feasible. She remained silent.

'I was astonished when I found you'd left the party. Surely you could have had the good manners to tell me of your intentions. It was hypocrisy, to say the least, to pretend you were so concerned about Melinda and then go off and spend at least two hours with Mike. Couldn't you have left that until tomorrow? I gather he still has a few days left of his holiday.'

She met his eyes, dark blue and accusing. What could she say?

'I'm sorry, Ross. I know how it must appear to you. I didn't think it would be considered ill-mannered. If I've let you down, I regret it.'

'It's a bit late for regrets. I don't understand you, Taryn. You've been difficult the whole evening. If you didn't want to come why did you not say so in the first place? Did you hate the whole thing? Why, you even refused to dance with me.'

She flinched as if he had hit her.

'I was sorry about that, but I had promised Mike.'

He broke in, sounding furious.

'I had really no idea that Mike had absorbed so much of your interest. But it's not too late for that dance. Put on the record player and we shall have it now. I'm not used to having anything refused me.'

'No, really, Ross, I think we should leave it. It's late and Melinda's asleep.'

'Nonsense, she won't wake. I shall put on the record and choose something soft and romantic. Isn't that what would please you?'

She watched him as he strode across to the record player and started it up with a slow glamorous tune that was sung by a voice like black velvet. He seemed so different from the calm enigmatic man she was used to. What was wrong? Had he quarrelled with Coral? Deep inside her she felt a quiver of fear. Yes, she was afraid to be alone with this dark stranger, afraid to surrender herself into the arms that were held invitingly open.

Earlier in the evening she would have given anything to have danced with him in the crowded ballroom, but this was different. She was afraid that if they danced together in this golden room, with its soft shadows and shaded glowing lamps, high above the sleeping city, she would betray the emotions that had come into her heart secretly and against her will.

But there was no retreat, no way she could refuse the silent command of his eyes that smouldered like the innermost flames of a fire and yet were as cold as ice. She was in his arms and they moved silently around the room. Once she stumbled a little and he held her closer. She shut her eyes, not able to encounter his burning glance.

'What is it? If you close your eyes, do you imagine you're dancing with Mike? Open them, Taryn. You're dancing with me, the dance you refused me this evening. Try to look as if you're enjoying it. Good God, why do you look so piteous? I'm not so much of an ogre to you – or am I? Why are you trembling? Are you afraid of me?'

Taryn shook her head. She could not speak. She was only deeply conscious of his hand at her waist, his dark head bending so close to hers.

'Do you dislike me so much? Is that why you refused to dance with me? Sometimes, Taryn, you act as if you hate me.'

She stopped dancing and attempted to break away from his grasp, but he held her firmly. She tried to speak calmly.

'Of course I don't hate you. You've been very good, very generous to me. I know all the time you've been dissatisfied. It's you who seemed always to dislike me.'

'That's not true. I've never felt that. I've had no feelings of that kind at all.'

She was deeply hurt. His tone seemed to imply that he had no thoughts about her, good or bad, that to him she had always been totally insignificant.

And yet his icy expression had gone. He seemed now as if he were bent on being as charming as possible. He smiled and his lips brushed her hair.

'Then, Taryn, if you don't hate me, why have you avoided the kiss you promised?'

'It was a joke, you know that. Completely unimportant to you.'

'Allow me to judge what's important to me. I saw you put your arms around Mike and kiss him before he'd even kissed you. Does he mean so much to you?'

'No, but that's different. He's not like you. You're my employer.'

His smile vanished.

'I understand. Thank you for explaining it to me. You've put me in my place. I'm your employer and not your friend it seems, quite unimportant compared with Mike. Good night, Taryn. I apologize for bothering you.'

He slammed out of the room, returning with his overnight bag. Taryn still stood as if paralysed where he had left her, but when released from his presence, she sank down into a chair, for her legs felt as if they could no longer function properly. When Ross came into the room again he barely glanced at her.

'I shall spend the night elsewhere. You would probably prefer that. I'm going to America, as you know, in a couple of days. You needn't see me again, Taryn. I shall arrange at the office that you're to have anything you need and that a car is to be sent to take Melinda to school. I suppose you won't be staying here much longer after that, but I repeat that if you need your fare home I shall leave instructions that you're to have it. Don't hesitate to claim it. However, I suppose you'll have other ideas now that you've met Mike again.'

She murmured some words of thanks. She had no intention of ever making any claim on him. She had saved while she was working and she would go to the room she had rented and look around for another job. At the moment she felt as if she never wanted to see anyone from Silver Ridge again, certainly not Ross.

CHAPTER TWELVE

SOMETIMES when Taryn came home late at night, tired out from her long hours in the coffee bar, where she was working, she saw the evening dress hanging in the shabby wardrobe of the small room and she smiled sadly, thinking what a different life she was leading now.

She had not seen Ross again after that night. Melinda had been very gentle and apologetic about the trouble she had caused, but of course she did not know that she had put Taryn so much in the wrong with Ross. Her love affair had been of short duration and it was a sadder and wiser girl who got into the hired car and went off to boarding school in her neat new uniform. Taryn had packed her small suitcase, tidied up the apartment, taken a long look around it, at the lovely room, the vast view of ocean and city, and then closed the door upon it, she thought, for ever.

She felt guilty about Mike, but she wanted to be on her own for a while. She did not want anyone to know what she was doing or where she was. She could never love Mike and he deserved better than to be kept hanging around while she agonized over Ross. For it was agony, and there was no mistaking that. Taryn missed him and thought of him all through the day, even though she was working harder than she had ever worked in her life before.

She had taken a job in a coffee bar in the city, a place that sold snacks, hamburgers, sausage rolls, toasted sandwiches. Even when Ross came back from America, he would never find her in a place like this. Not that she expected he would look for her, but they would never meet here by accident, for it was the last place where she would expect to see him.

Her uniform was supplied to her and her room was not very expensive. Her meals were free, so she saved quite a lot of her pay. She thought perhaps when she had enough she would fly back to England. She would never claim the passage money that Ross had promised her. She felt she had been a disappointment to him from first to last. Perhaps it would be a good thing if she went back home. But what was there to which she could return?

Perhaps she had been wrong not to keep in touch with Mike, but she fought her impulse to write and tell him where she was working. She knew she should not do it, when really she did not have the feeling for him that he desired. It was loneliness that made her feel weak. The days were not so bad. She would be rushed off her feet taking orders, preparing snacks, trying to be pleasant to the large variety of customers.

But at night she would return in a crowded bus to her lonely room above the city, where she would do her various chores and prepare for the next day's work, physically tired out but mentally restless. Then thoughts and dreams would come crowding in and she would look at the high ridge where the penthouse stood, and think of it, dark and deserted, now that Ross was in America.

Often one of the regular customers would start chatting to her and occasionally they tried to date her, but she always refused.

'You're crazy,' said Linda, the other girl at the counter. 'What's the idea? Why don't you want an outing now and then? Have you got a steady somewhere?'

'Yes, I have, but he's overseas,' Taryn replied.

She hated to lie, but she thought this would perhaps solve her problem, and it did. Linda, glad to divert attention to herself, was eager to tell the young men who displayed interest in Taryn that she was engaged, or almost, and they accepted this and stopped asking her out.

She felt bad about not writing to Melinda, and finally wrote a letter but gave the number of the postal box that the manager of the coffee bar rented. Melinda wrote back saying that school was not so bad. She had made the second hockey team and the work was not impossible.

'It seems an awful long time to have to wait until the holidays. I do hope you'll still be there in Durban. What are you doing? You didn't tell me. You'll be glad to know that I've finished with Donald. That last evening showed me what he was like. Perhaps you were right and I'm too young for a boy-friend yet.'

Taryn thought she would not see Melinda again. She had deliberately chosen to put all that life behind her. Perhaps she could manage a week-end at a mountain resort, not anywhere near Silver Ridge but just somewhere to remind her of how much she had loved that wild country. But no, perhaps better not. It would bring back too many bitter memories. She wondered whether to go to some other place, Cape Town or Johannesburg perhaps. There she would be certain of never meeting anyone from her past. But, living on her own, she was like a small mouse in its hole. She had got used to it now and felt a certain amount of security. At present she could not face going to a strange place and making a new life all over again so soon after she had established herself here, even if she knew it was rather temporary and precarious.

She could not forget how she had felt during those first lonely days; waking up each morning in the commonplace little room, she would feel a heaviness that she knew was in her mind but seemed to affect her whole body. She would close her eyes again, overcome with a sickness of grief, but then, dragging herself from her bed, she would make tea and drink it down until the heat brought some relief to the terrible empty pain.

In the street, even now sometimes, she would think she caught sight of Ross, his dear dark head tall above the crowd, and then she would want to run to him, to plead with him that he should take her back, that she would work for him, do anything for him so long as she could see him occasionally and not be banished completely into this ghastly loneliness. But then she would see that she was mistaken, and the sensible side of her would be glad.

So the weeks dragged by and the long hot summer eventually turned into autumn, but a kind of autumn that she had never known before, cooler nights but sparkling sunlit days, no falling leaves but shrubs bursting into blossom as if it were midsummer. She had not replied to Melinda's letter, for what could she say? She would have to lie to her by saying she was going away, because she was not prepared to meet her during the holidays. So she left it and doubtless Melinda felt hurt, but it was better so.

She had had a shock one day shortly after she had written to Melinda, when the manager said to her,

'Hi, Taryn, someone is inquiring about you. This fellow has written to my box number asking if I know anything about you.'

He showed it to her and she realized it was from Mike. He must have got the number from Melinda.

'I should prefer it if you didn't reply, or better still write and say there must be some mistake,' Taryn asked.

'It's your own affair. I'll do that for you.'

For a while she was nervous about this and then, as nothing happened, she thought Mike had given up trying to find her. Obviously she did not want anything from him, so surely he would not persist. The work in the coffee bar, though fairly congenial, was exhausting, with long hours. Taryn, never very fat, became thinner than ever and her brown eyes looked huge in a face that had lost its honey tan from all the long hours spent indoors, often over hot stoves.

One day it seemed to have been particularly tiring. Everything had gone wrong from the very start. There had been a power cut and they had had to mop up the pools from the melted ice. The cheese had gone mouldy, the bread rolls were delivered late, and something had gone wrong with the coffee percolating machines. During this time between summer and winter, people often objected to the cool air-conditioning in the place and it was hotter here than in midsummer, not to the customers, for they were sitting in comfort, but not so nice for the assistants who had to dash around getting food from the warming ovens. Taryn was helping in the hot kitchen, her hair screwed up on top of her head, her face shiny, when a waitress came in and said, 'Someone's at the counter asking for you.'

'Oh, no, tell him I'm not here.'

She knew instinctively that it was Mike.

'I've already told him you're here. I'm sorry.'

Taryn walked slowly out of the kitchen. It was not the end of the world, she assured herself, that Mike had found her. She would ask him not to tell anyone else. She was surprised by the surge of happiness that she felt when she saw the bright red dishevelled hair and the craggy frame.

'Mike, how did you find me?'

'You may well ask. I've had the devil's own job. You might have written to me – I've been nearly out of my mind with worry wondering what had happened to you.'

'I'm sorry, Mike, but I thought it was for the best.'

'What have they done to you? You look terrible,' he said frankly. His blue eyes were very concerned, very kind.

'I'm all right. I'm fine. Mike, I can't talk now. We're frightfully busy, as you can see.'

'What time do you get off? I'll wait for you.'

Taryn arranged to meet him after work. She was reluctant to let Mike know where she was living, so they sat in his car on the promenade watching the sea splashing its white foam over the rocks.

'I have to go back tomorrow,' he said. 'I found out the box number by a trick and traced you to the coffee bar. Why did you disappear out of my life, Taryn?'

'It seemed best at the time, Mike. I wanted to get away, to be on my own.'

'If I could offer you a job again at the camp, would you take it now?'

'No, I don't think so.'

'I thought you loved the mountains.'

'I do, Mike, but it's no use. I can't come back.'

'Is it Ross? Did he upset you in some way? Because if it's that, I can assure you you won't see him there. He's in America, but in any case he hasn't been to Silver Ridge since the children left.'

'I can't tell you, Mike. I just want to close off that part of my life for ever.'

'Taryn, give me another chance,' he begged. 'Come to the camp for the week-end. I promise I won't worry you and that you won't have to go near Silver Ridge. Ross is still in America, so even if you have quarrelled with him, you won't see him. It would do you good to get away for a day or two. You look all in.'

As it happened it was Taryn's week-end off from the next day. They were allowed one Friday a month added to a free week-end because of the long hours they worked at other times. She thought of the hours she would have to spend in the lonely room or the time she would have to spend on her own walking around the city or the beaches. She was sick with loneliness, tired of the time spent dreaming and yearning for Ross. Mike's offer was very tempting.

'All right, I'll come,' she said. 'But only for the week-end.'

They set out early on Friday morning. Taryn, still wary about letting Mike know where she stayed, got a bus into the town and met him at the terminus. In Durban, autumn had come without any noticeable change from the usual lush green of foliage, but as they made their way inland the Natal Midlands were transformed by their autumn colours, the crops gathered in, the maize fields rid of their tasselled heads and left with faded stubble amongst which the oxen grazed. In the gardens, plane trees shed their brown-gold leaves. The long summer had ended.

'This time of the year should tempt you back if anything will,' said Mike. 'It's crisp but not too cold. The snow comes later. But this is the time that worries me for my eland. There's enough grazing in summer but not sufficient in winter. At least, that's the conclusion I seem to be coming to from my survey.'

Taryn was so tired that she slept for a good part of the way, rousing herself, however, when the first blue mountains came into view. She had thought she would never see this part of the world again, and here she was, thrilling to the sight of the wild scenery. But Ross would not be there. It would be strange to go to the camp and not visit Silver Ridge, but she was determined she would not even go near the house. In any case there would only be the new house-keeper there. The boys had gone to school long ago and Allister had taken another post.

They arrived at the camp in time for lunch. Mike had

phoned and arranged that Taryn should stay with the super-intendent and his wife, and they made her very welcome.

'It's good of you to have me at such short notice,' said Taryn.

'That's no trouble. Mike will entertain you and you'll eat with him. I expect you'll both be out most of the time. Our daughter has gone overseas, so it's good to have someone young around again. Mike's a good fellow – but I'm probably telling you something you know already.'

She and Mike had a simple lunch at his cottage and afterwards it was obvious to him that she could hardly keep her eyes open.

'Go and rest, Taryn,' he said. 'It's clear that you've been under some kind of strain. Isn't that job too much for you? I don't know why you took it. Surely you could have found something easier?'

'It's hard, but the people are very kind,' Taryn told him. 'It's no one's fault but my own that I'm so terribly . . .' she broke off, for she had been going to say 'lonely' and she did not want to admit that to Mike.

'Terribly what?' His kind blue eyes were full of concern for her.

'Nothing really. Terribly tired, I suppose I was going to say,' she admitted with a yawn. 'I think I'll rest, Mike. Sorry to be such bad company.'

'That's fine with me. Have a good sleep this afternoon. There's a bit of a braai and a hop tonight in the shed. And tomorrow I wondered if you'd like to go up the mountain to a hide where you can watch the eagles and lammergeiers.'

'Oh, that would be wonderful, but I hardly feel capable of climbing a mountain.'

'You won't have to. I'll take you there in my four-wheel-drive truck. I won't be able to stay with you, because I have to go up to the hut further up the mountain, and in any case the birds won't come to feed if they see a vehicle there. I'll call back for you when I think you've had enough. Will you be scared to be alone on the mountain?'

'No, of course not. And I shall know you're coming back for me soon. I'm longing to see those marvellous eagles at closer quarters.'

'It will be quite safe, of course. They won't even see you. You'll be in the hide and we'll take fresh bones to attract them to feed.'

Taryn spent the whole afternoon sleeping. She had not realized how tired she had become until she had come here. She awoke refreshed for the braai and dance that was to be held that evening. The nights were cold now, so Mrs. Fairhurst advised her that the girls would be wearing casual slacks and shirts. She put on the brown slacks and striped jersey she had bought for the Zululand game reserve trip. Already she looked prettier, her colour more radiant, her hair shining. When Mike called for her, he smiled, 'You look just as beautiful to me, Taryn, in that outfit as you did in that wonderful dress.'

It was clear that the others regarded her as Mike's girl. They made her welcome and seemed to take it for granted that they would see her again. Had she been wise, she wondered, to come here at all? She had tried hard not to think of Ross or to look in the direction of Silver Ridge.

'I've been told you were working for Ross Trent before you went to Durban,' one girl said when Mike had gone off to grill the meat. 'That must have been exciting.'

'He looks quite gorgeous,' said another girl, joining in the conversation. 'They say it won't be long before he marries Coral Swann. She's planning the wedding already. I don't suppose he'll come here often after that.'

There was nothing in this conversation that was news to Taryn, so why did it threaten to mar her carefully balanced good spirits? She smiled at Mike as he came back balancing a paper plate laden with chops and sausages done on the coals, determined not to spoil his evening by feeling depressed. So for the rest of the time she tried to appear gay and charming, but Mike, it appeared, was not deceived. The moon was silvering the grass as they walked back to the camp. A huge ring spread in a circle around it.

'Ice crystals,' Mike explained. 'It sometimes means snow, but it's rather early in the season for that, I think.'

He took her arm to guide her over a rough place in the

path, saying, 'You haven't minded coming here, Taryn?'

'Oh, Mike, you know I love this part of the country.'

'Can't you love me as well?'

She shook her head.

'I wish I could, Mike. But at the moment I'm not sure of any of my feelings at all. I seem to be rather numb.'

'Why? You look so unhappy when you think no one is looking. Tell me, Taryn, did Ross charm you as he appears to attract all women? Is that it?'

It was a shock to hear Mike say so frankly what he was thinking. Tears sprang to her eyes and started to roll down her cheeks. Mike put his arm round her and stopped walking.

'Taryn, my dear, I didn't mean to upset you. Is it as bad as that?'

She used the handkerchief he offered.

'I shall get over it. I shall have to, won't I?'

'I was a fool to ask you back here. It's probably made you sad again. Believe me, he isn't worth it.'

'I've been sad for a long time,' she sighed. 'But I shall get over it in time. I'll go back to England and forget Silver Ridge and these mountains ever existed.'

'Don't do that. You could be happy here with me. See how you feel about it tomorrow when you've had a good night's sleep.'

She woke next morning, feeling strangely peaceful. For so long she had awakened to a feeling of misery that she could not at first understand what had happened. But here in this little room with its basic furniture and its white walls, thatched roof and wooden beams, she felt at home once more. There was an odd light reflecting on the small window, and while she was wondering about this, though feeling deliciously drowsy, Mrs. Fairhurst came in with the coffee.

'You've brought the snow with you,' she exclaimed cheerfully. 'The first fall of the winter.'

She drew the curtain and there was the range with a white blanket on the top reaching half-way down.

'Won't we be able to go up to the hide?' asked Taryn,

fascinated by the view but regretting their proposed expedition.

'I think you can go. It's just a slight fall and by the time you get there it will probably be melted. The four-wheel-drive vehicles can cope with most weather.'

Mike was of the same opinion when he called for her. Mrs. Fairhurst had provided Taryn with a weatherproof jacket with a hood and she wore her warmest slacks and jersey.

'I'm so glad you're taking me up the mountain,' she told Mike. He was wearing a greatcoat, and his face was reddened by the wind, for the truck was small and open.

'You mustn't expect very luxurious travelling,' he warned.

They drove along a rough track which finally disappeared, and they were on the open grasslands of the mountain. Swerving and bumping, they made their way upwards. The wind was icy in the open vehicle, and Taryn was glad of the woollen muffler wound around the lower part of her face. They had brought a sack of fresh bones to feed the great birds, and Mike strode over to a rock and distributed them around. He indicated the hide some way off across the rocks.

'I won't come with you. The sooner I go the sooner I shall be back. The birds will keep away for a while because they've seen the truck, but they'll soon be tempted by the bones.'

Taryn stood watching the truck disappearing around into the next valley. It was not so cold here as it had been while travelling in the truck, but she would be glad to get into the hide. All around her the mountains unfolded tier upon tier of snowcapped sweeping countryside. Below the ground fell away into a ravine, and she could see some birds wide-winged and effortlessly soaring. It seemed so strange that they were below her.

She remembered the first time she had seen a black eagle high above her, and how Ross had flung his head back to look at it and she had thought he was like the bird, wild and free.

'Taryn!'

The voice was surely conjured up from her imagination, because she had been thinking of him.

'Taryn!'

It was no ghost voice. It was the voice she knew so well, strong and vibrant.

'For God's sake, girl, come into the hide, otherwise the birds will never come.'

She walked the few yards to the structure that was made of wood with no window save a narrow slit for viewing. A few steps led to the door. Ross was waiting at the top, and as she came up, he put out his hand to help her in. There was a large notice on the wall, 'Silence', and he pointed at this, shaking his head and drawing her down to sit beside him on the small narrow seat.

'Don't look so startled,' he whispered. 'Where did you spring from, Taryn?'

'I might ask the same of you,' she whispered back. 'I thought you were in America.'

'I cut my visit short. Now don't say another word. The birds have seen the bones.'

He put his hand over hers and pointed to the place a few yards away where Mike had deposited them. A young lammergeier, a bearded vulture, had landed and was cautiously approaching the food. It had a golden head and dark brown wings but was still a little fluffy underneath. Two black crows, shining and sleek, tried to head it off with their fierce yellow beaks. Then a larger bearded vulture arrived and with fury and outstretched talons drove away the crows. The young one hovered on the edge, but finding it was not attacked any more proceeded to feed.

'Take my binoculars,' Ross whispered, and, putting them into her hands, held them steady while she gazed at the birds, which now seemed only a few feet away.

'Are you cold?' he asked. She shook her head. 'Then why are you trembling?'

Taryn could not speak, but felt that if she did she would do something foolish like bursting into tears. She concentrated on watching the birds and yet felt a great surge of joy that she was here with Ross, whom she had thought she would never see again.

'Why did Mike leave you here alone?' he asked.

'He's coming back for me. He went to the mountain hut higher up. How did you get here?'

'I walked, of course. Look, here come the eagles.'

They dropped out of the skies, the fierce black birds with their uncanny yellow eyes, their horny yellowish beaks showing up against the black heads. They landed with a rocking movement of their broad grey and black wings and took no notice of any of the other birds, majestically ignoring a pair of falcons which, although so much smaller, seemed inclined to harass them.

'Oh, they're beautiful!' she breathed. 'Even when they're fighting for food. But it's when they're soaring above the hills that they're most majestic.'

'Here come some more lammergeiers. The older ones are very shy. There are few left now. Their numbers are decreasing because they can't find carrion any more, and that's their natural food, of course.'

For a while they both watched the birds in silence. What did it matter, thought Taryn, if this happiness was to last for such a little while? She was here on the mountain with Ross, a thing she had never expected and would have dreaded if she had known it was to happen, but now, in this snowy landscape, watching the fierce, glorious birds with him at her side, she felt the surging joy that had first come to her when she saw the black eagle in flight and looked at Ross with his face upturned to the skies admiring the proud, arrogant bird.

The eagle and bearded vultures that were still circling above the rocks caught the currents of air in graceful effortless flight, then landed on the rocks, strutting so grandly as if they owned this part of the world. But after some while they ceased their eating, for the bones were demolished. Only a few peregrine falcons remained, trying to find a little morsel that had perhaps been overlooked.

'It's still a joy to me to watch your face when you see anything that's new to you, Taryn,' Ross said softly.

She looked at him and met the intense gaze of his dark blue eyes with their fringe of black heavy lashes.

'You're supposed to be watching the eagles and lammergeiers, not me, Ross,' she replied.

'I do whatever gives me the most pleasure,' he said. 'But there, Taryn, I mustn't say such things, must I? Mike wouldn't like it.'

'You make me so angry!' she exclaimed. 'Why do you feel you have to flatter any woman when you find yourself alone with her?'

'I find it pays,' he said, unabashed. 'Don't all women love flattery?'

'Not at all,' she said. 'Some like men to be truthful and sincere.'

'Like Mike,' he said. 'Oh, yes, Taryn, I can see you need an honest Joe type like him. I always told you so, didn't I?'

'And I told you that I didn't need any interference in my own affairs,' Taryn retorted.

She was exasperated now and did not care what she said. He laughed delightedly.

'I like to see you angry, Taryn my darling. It's quite a change.'

'I'm not your darling, and I have no wish to be!'

'Being cross with me has stopped your shivering and put the roses back into your cheeks. A good thing too, because although I hate to have to tell you this, Taryn, I'm afraid you're going to have to walk home with me.'

'What do you mean? Mike's coming back for me.'

'I doubt it. I've been watching his truck on the mountain in between looking at more interesting sights, and you can take my word for it he's well and truly stuck. But there's no need for alarm. He can stay in the hut. There's a heater and supplies there. We'll leave him a note here to say we've started to go down the mountain.'

'I'd prefer to wait here for him,' Taryn insisted.

'And I'd prefer that you came with me. The sooner we get down the better. Look at those clouds coming over the mountain.'

The weather had changed. The clear blue sky had been replaced by grey clouds and wisps of mist were gathering over the peaks.

'More snow,' said Ross.

'But Mike will be worried about me,' protested Taryn. 'He won't just stay up in the hut knowing I'm here.'

'Then he'll have to walk down after he finds our note. He's used to these conditions and he's tough. You're not, Taryn. We must get you back as soon as we can. We'll report back to the camp as soon as we get to Silver Ridge.'

'I'm not coming to Silver Ridge with you!'

'Why ever not? It's the nearest house. Now stop fussing, Taryn, and let's be on our way.'

Outside the hide, the wind was strong and bitterly cold.

'Do you know the way down?' asked Taryn fearfully.

'Of course I do, girl, I came up, didn't I? Unfortunately the track is along the ridge and we can expect the full force of the wind. That's why I said we must get down quickly.'

They had not been walking very long before it began to snow, small soft flakes at first, scarcely noticeable, and then it became worse, frosting their eyes with icy fingers and penetrating the muffler that Taryn wore over the lower part of her face, making it damp and uncomfortable. Ross was wearing a waterproof jacket, but both of them found they had to keep moving quickly to prevent their legs getting numb, for the icy wind on the ridge seemed to penetrate through their clothing.

They turned around a curve of the track and suddenly the full force of the gale broke upon them. Taryn was almost blown off her feet and Ross had to hold her while they stood swaying together.

'I'm sorry I got you into this,' he shouted. His arms were around her trying to stem the force of the bitter wind. 'But we could hardly have stayed in the hide. We would have frozen without any activity.'

On they went, slipping, sliding along the rough track that was covered with mud and snow, sometimes leaving it and battling over the wet grassy slopes to try to take a short cut. Once they found a place in a hollow that was sheltered from the gale, and here Ross held her close.

'Do you want to stay here and I'll go on?' he asked. 'You could shelter between these rocks out of the wind and I can send a vehicle for you.'

'No, I'll go on.'

'Good girl!' He still had his arms around her. 'Do you remember that night when we rode out of the gorge? It wasn't as uncomfortable as this, was it?'

She shook her head. That was the night when she had first come to love him, she thought, although she had not realized it until much later. It was odd that he should have mentioned it now.

They struggled on for what seemed a long time. Sometimes she thought maybe it would have been better to stay in the shelter of the rocks, but she could not have let Ross go on on his own. She was determined to see this through to the end, although she was almost fainting with exhaustion. She lost count of time, but it seemed like hours as they plodded on, half frozen. Was it her imagination, was she just getting used to this terrible path, or had it become easier? And there were lights through the haze of mist and snow, lights up on that slope.

'We've made it!' Ross shouted, his voice hoarse and jubilant. 'A little way and we'll be at Silver Ridge. Taryn, my love, you were terrific!'

The words lingered with her while she went to her old room and had a hot bath. Mrs. Brown, the new housekeeper, fussed over her, bringing her some old denim jeans of Melinda's and the Aran pullover belonging to Ross. It was of course miles too big and the rolled collar made her face and neck look thinner than ever. She came shyly into the living room. How wonderful it was to see it again. And there was a log fire roaring in the stone fireplace. She knelt down on the hearthrug, still glad of the heat of the flames in spite of the hot bath and the warm jersey.

She had not heard when Ross came into the room. She was only aware of him when he took her hands and pulled her to her feet, then led her to sit on the settee beside him.

'Mike's fine. He came down the mountain by a shorter

path after he'd found our note. He had to leave the truck at the mountain hut, but they'll send for it later. I told you he's pretty tough. He'll make a good husband for any girl.'

'For any girl, yes, I agree.'

'You're smiling,' commented Ross. 'I believe you're teasing me. Surely you intend to marry Mike? But I forgot, it's none of my business.'

He was looking at her and there was something quite different now about the expression of those dark blue eyes, something she had sensed, since they had come together, almost as one person, fighting against the storm. It was odd that now she was no longer nervous of encountering that intense blue gaze. She felt at ease with him, free to say anything.

'Mike's a dear person and will make a good husband for someone else, Ross. But not for me. I've told him so.'

She hesitated for a moment and then said, 'Now it's my turn. Surely you intend to marry Coral? But that's not my business either, is it?'

'Coral is very much involved with Brad and I'm not shedding any tears over her, Taryn. And it certainly is your business. At least I'm hoping so.'

Slowly he put his hand under her chin and turned her face towards him.

'You're wonderful, Taryn, you were so brave and courageous on that bitter walk down the mountain. I always knew you were completely adorable, but I didn't know you had such courage as well.'

She gazed into his eyes unable to believe his words, but the expression in the dark blue depths of them told her that he was sincere.

'Adorable?' she stammered.

'Don't you realize that I adore you, worship you, that I've loved you for a very long time, ever since that night when we rode out of the gorge and you'd injured your ankle? You were great then, but you've been even more wonderful today. I came back from America because I had to find you again, but when I heard you'd come to the camp with Mike, I was convinced that you loved him. I was trying to work out my despair when I walked up the mountain this morning.'

'Oh, Ross, I never loved Mike. Only you.'

'I can't believe it, but your eyes, those lovely, lovely eyes, tell me you're speaking the truth. Could you marry me, Taryn?'

'Do you know what you're saying, Ross?' asked Taryn. 'We won't spend all the days of our lives walking through snowstorms or riding out of the Gorge. I'm not sophisticated. I'm not beautiful.'

'You're lovely,' he said. 'You're everything I ever wanted in a woman. Dear, sweet Taryn, say we can spend all the days of our lives together, with or without snowstorms.'

'Oh, Ross, my sweet love, my dear love, I'd like nothing better in all the world,' said Taryn, and knew that she was to have this happiness for ever.

January paperbacks

THE MOON FOR LAVINIA *by Betty Neels*
Lavinia's husband only wanted a housekeeper—but what about Lavinia?

NO JUST CAUSE *by Susan Barrie*
Why should rich, handsome James be interested in quiet little Carole?

SMOKE INTO FLAME *by Jane Arbor*
For the second time Clare had fallen in love with an Italian—who didn't want her!

THE WILDERNESS HUT *by Mary Wibberley*
Eve was a rich girl, Garth Seton the pilot she had hired—a man who didn't jump to anyone's bidding . . .

WHITE ROSE OF LOVE *by Anita Charles*
Steve felt she resembled a red rose—but Dom Manoel made it clear that he preferred white ones!

THE HUNGRY TIDE *by Lucy Gillen*
Rachel's small charge gave her no trouble. No, the problem was his two uncles . . .

RETURN TO TUCKARIMBA *by Amanda Doyle*
Nonie wanted to buy back her childhood home, but the owner had other ideas!

VALLEY OF PARADISE *by Margaret Rome*
Serena went to Chile—to a husband she had never met.

WHERE THE SOUTH WIND BLOWS *by Anne Hampson*
Would Melanie's unscrupulous sister break up her romance for the *third* time?

THE GARDEN OF DREAMS *by Sara Craven*
Did Lissa want to marry Paul de Gue or not?

30p net each
Available January 1976

Look out for the Mills & Boon 1975 Pack
Available now!

THE DEVIL'S DARLING
by Violet Winspear

'But you don't know me—you don't love me,' Persepha protested when the magnetic Don Diablo Ezreldo Ruy announced his intention of marrying her. 'In Mexico, *señorita*, the knowing and the loving come after marriage,' he told her. But would they?

COME THE VINTAGE
by Anne Mather

Ryan's father had left her a half share of his prosperous vine-growing business, and the other half to a man she had never heard of, a Frenchman named Alain de Beaunes—on condition that they married each other. So, for the sake of the business, they married, neither caring anything for the other. Where did they go from there?

FLAME OF FATE
by Anne Hampson

It was years since Alana had seen Conon Mavilis, although she knew he still hated her for having turned him down. Now, in Greece, they had met again, and Conon, smouldering and embittered, was insisting that she become his wife. And this time he had the power to make her agree ...

DARK INTRUDER
by Nerina Hilliard

Young Kerry Derwin didn't want this film unit intruding into her peaceful, happy life and turning it upside down. And she wasn't interested in the star, Paul Devron, either. Certainly she wasn't going to add herself to his long list of conquests. But then Kerry hadn't yet actually met Paul Devron ...

£1.20 net

Your Mills & Boon selection!

Over the page we have listed a number of titles which we feel you may have missed or had difficulty in obtaining from your local bookshop over the past months. If you can see some titles you would like to add to your Mills & Boon collection, just tick your selection, fill in the coupon below and send the whole page to us with your remittance including postage and packing. We will despatch your order to you by return!

If you would like a complete list of all the Mills & Boon romances which are currently available either from your local bookshop or, if in difficulty, direct from Mills & Boon Reader Service, together with details of all the forthcoming publications and special offers, why not fill in the coupon below and you will receive, by return and post free, your own copy of the Mills & Boon catalogue—Happy Reading. Why not send for your copy today?

To: MILLS & BOON READER SERVICE, P.O. BOX 236, 14 Sanderstead Road, South Croydon, Surrey CR2 0YG, England

Please send me the titles ticked   ☐

Please send me the free Mills & Boon Magazine   ☐

I enclose £..................................(No C.O.D.) Please add 5p per book—standard charge of 25p per order when you order five or more paperbacks. (15p per paperback if you live outside the UK).

Name.. Miss/Mrs

Address ....

City/Town ....

County/Country.......................Postal/Zip Code......................

Will South African and Rhodesian readers please write to: P.O. BOX 11190, JOHANNESBURG 2000, SOUTH AFRICA. NEW TITLES only available from this address.

MB 12/75

Your Mills & Boon Selection!

☐ 002
MY TENDER FURY
Margaret Malcolm

☐ 007
THE THIRD UNCLE
Sara Seale

☐ 133
INHERIT MY HEART
Mary Burchell

☐ 203
KINGFISHER TIDE
Jane Arbor

☐ 255
PARADISE ISLAND
Hilary Wilde

☐ 293
HOTEL BY THE LOCH
Iris Danbury

☐ 307
THE DREAM AND THE
DANCER
Eleanor Franes

☐ 336
PEPPERCORN HARVEST
Ivy Ferrari

☐ 900
THE WARM WIND OF FARIK
Rebecca Stratton

☐ 927
WITCHSTONE
Anne Mather

☐ 935
THE SNOW ON THE HILLS
Mary Wibberley

☐ 944
SWEET ROOTS AND HONEY
Gwen Westwood

☐ 950
DANGEROUS TO KNOW
Elizabeth Ashton

☐ 957
DARLING JENNY
Janet Dailey

☐ 962
AUTUMN CONCERTO
Rebecca Stratton

☐ 967
HEAVEN IS GENTLE
Betty Neels

☐ 972
THE SMOKE AND THE FIRE
Essie Summers

☐ 977
RETURN TO DEEPWATER
Lucy Gillen

☐ 982
NO ORCHIDS BY REQUEST
Essie Summers

☐ 987
A PAVEMENT OF PEARL
Iris Danbury

☐ 993
FIRE AND ICE
Janet Dailey

☐ 998
DANGEROUS RHAPSODY
Anne Mather

☐ 1003
THE FARAWAY BRIDE
Linden Grierson

☐ 1008
RIDE OUT THE STORM
Jane Donnelly

☐ 1013
THE WIDE FIELDS OF HOME
Jane Arbor

All priced at 25p. Please tick your requirements and use the
handy order form overleaf.